SUMMER VACATION

SUMMER VACATION

Published by BHC Press
under the Barking Frog imprint

Library of Congress Control Number:
2018946377

ISBN: 978-1-947727-72-4

Also available in ebook

Visit the publisher at:
www.bhcpress.com

OTHER BOOKS IN

THE ── CHILDHOOD LEGENDS® ──SERIES──

BY JUDITH BLEVINS & CARROLL MULTZ

Operation Cat Tale

One Frightful Day

Blue

The Ghost of Bradbury Mansion

White Out

A Flash of Red

Back in Time

Treasure Seekers

TABLE OF CONTENTS

PART ONE - CASTAWAYS

PART TWO - BLAST OFF

AUTHORS' NOTE

Like most of you we could hardly wait for summer vacation to begin when we were in school. It meant we had another grade behind us and three months away from the drudgery of classes. No homework to worry about and days filled with fun. We had chores at home and some of us had outside jobs that took our minds off school and gave us an opportunity to earn spending money.

Some of us made trips to exotic places. Those in the mountain states traveled to states that had beaches and those who lived near the ocean traveled to the mountains. The occasional trips to Disney Land, Disney World, Yellowstone Park or Glacier Park were also memorable. Some summers were more memorable than others.

Summer Vacation is about a summer that several of the main characters of the R*U*1*2s will not soon forget. Part One entitled Castaways is about a harrowing experience at sea when Genius and Tank find themselves shipwrecked on a desolate island and rescued by pirates. Part Two entitled Blast Off finds Shacoo, Sally, Genius and Tank aboard a space ship orbiting Earth.

Our special thanks to Margie Vollmer Rabdau and our publisher, BHC Press for their technical skills and assistance.

TO OUR INSPIRATION

Cole, Emily, Joey, Kate, Kirsten,
Logan, Taran, Trenton, Bridget,
Hannah, Irina and Caroline

THE
CHILDHOOD LEGENDS®
SERIES

SUMMER VACATION

BY JUDITH BLEVINS
& CARROLL MULTZ

BARKING
FROG

LIVONIA, MICHIGAN

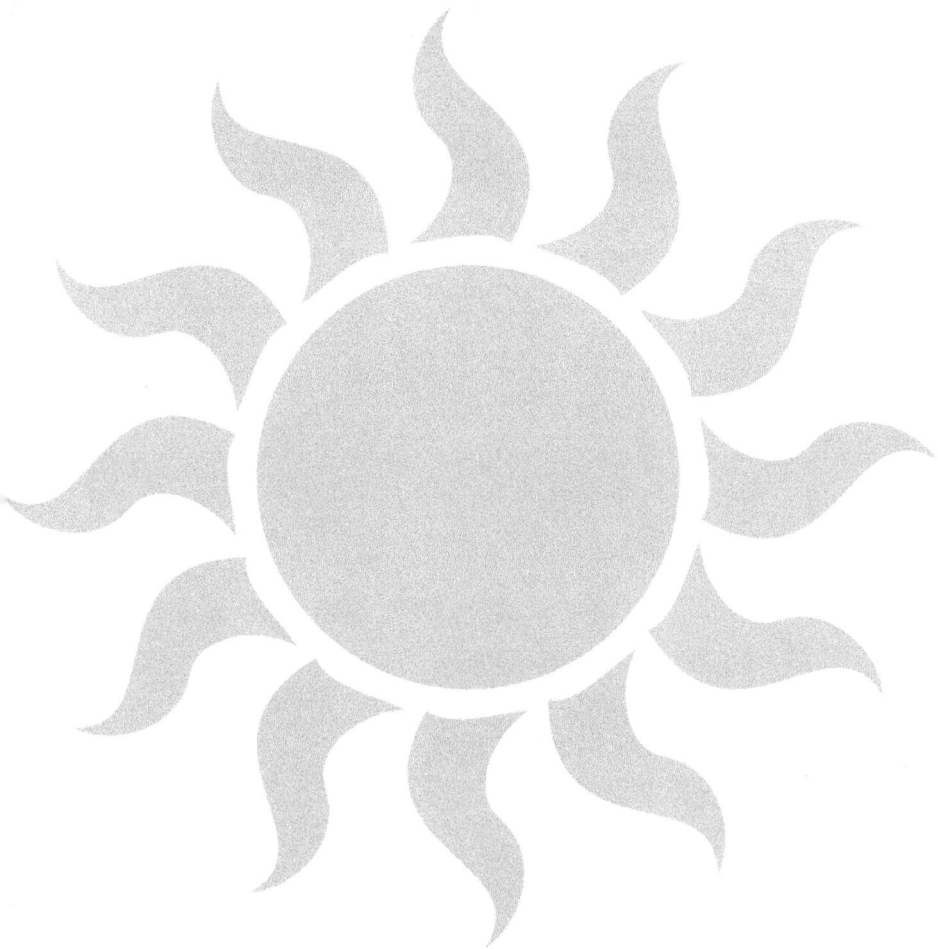

PART ONE
CASTAWAYS

CHAPTER ONE

THE JOURNEY BEGINS

My name is Robert Princeton Bailey. I live in Jefferson City, Iowa, and I go by the name of Genius. In the event this is the first novel you've read about the *R*U*1*2s*, I'll tell you a little bit about my background. I'm twelve years old and am an only child. Both my parents are medical doctors and lead a very busy life in a town that has very few doctors. I'm part of a youth group known as the *R*U*1*2s* and spend most of my free time at our clubhouse which is a renovated bunkhouse in the middle of an apple orchard owned by the parents of our youngest member, Rhymin' Sally. There are approximately two dozen members in our club.

It is not often my parents can take time away from their medical practice for family excursions. So when Dad suggests we spend two weeks with his brother and family in San Diego, California, I'm the first to get packed. My cousins Blake and Brandon are identical twins two years older than me and are the brothers I never had. The last time I saw them was two years ago when my parents celebrated my tenth birthday by taking me to Disney Land in Anaheim.

"Can Tank go with us?" I ask my parents. Tank is the nickname for one of my classmates and best friends. His real name is Timothy Patrick O'Malley. He earned his nickname because he is muscular and big for his age. He, together with another of our classmates Shacoo Bandaris, are charter members of the *R*U*1*2s*. We've been referred to as "the three musketeers" because of our close association.

"Of course he can," Dad says. "Assuming Tank's parents agree. They included you in their trip last summer to Yellowstone Park."

I'm immediately punching up Tank's cellphone number.

"Am I late for the *R*U*1*2s'* Arbor Day project at Jefferson City Public Park?" Tank asks.

"No! That's not for another hour yet. I have something great to tell you!"

"Your parents have doubled your allowance."

"Something even better."

"They've tripled it?"

"Tank, we're going to spend two weeks in San Diego with my uncle and aunt and cousins Blake and Brandon. They're the ones with the yacht."

"Great! Do you have a trunk big enough to smuggle me in?"

"You don't need to be a stowaway. My parents said you were invited!"

"Mom," Tank yells without covering the mouthpiece. "Genius and his parents want me to go to San Diego with them. Can I go? Please!"

"When is it?" I hear his mother yell back.

"When is it?" Tank asks me.

"Second week in June," I reply.

"Second week in June," he yells.

"We'll have to talk to your father when he comes home for dinner," I hear his mother say.

That evening my father gets a call from Tank's father. "Jackson, Liam O'Malley here. Tank tells me he received a call from Genius inviting him to travel with your family to San Diego. You know how much Tank loves boats and the sea."

"We'd love to have him join us," I hear my father say. Dad has a habit of talking on a speaker phone so that he doesn't have to hold the phone to his ear. He says that's because he's on the phone so much with his patients that the phone would be growing out of his ear without a speaker feature.

"That's very kind of you. Tank is adamant about going and reminded us how much fun it was last summer when Genius travelled with us to Yellowstone Park."

"They're joined at the hips," my Dad says. "It should be a fun trip. My brother Darrell actually lives in Coronado and we'd be staying with him and his family on the beach right next to the ocean."

"I was stationed at the Naval Amphibious Base on Coronado Island when I was in the Navy. Your brother is living in a high rent district it sounds like. He must be a doctor, too."

"No, he's a real estate salesman turned investor who unlike myself buys low and sells high. He's also a former Navy man."

"You say he lives on the beach?"

"Near the Pacific Ocean. That's why Genius loves going to visit Uncle Darrell and Aunt Lynnette and of course his cousins Blake and Brandon. We spend most of our time on Darrell's yacht. That's why Olivia and I make Genius wear a hat and several layers of sunscreen when we're at sea. We'll make sure Tank does the same."

"I learned the value of sunscreen," Liam says. "Boy, didn't I! When I was first in the Navy I had a burn that took a fire extinguisher to put out."

WITH SCHOOL OUT FOR the summer all I could think of was our trip to California. I wanted to buy some fancy swim trunks and t-shirts to take with me. Wisely I waited to buy them in California where I could purchase the latest rage and when I returned to Jefferson City show them off to the other *R*U*1*2s*.

"Thanks for offering to take me with you," Shacoo says snidely to Tank and me when she learns of the proposed trip. "You know how I like the ocean!"

"This is just for the guys," I say. "Besides you'd get bored swimming in the ocean every day, playing on the sandy beach and travelling across the waves of the Pacific Ocean on a yacht while the dolphins scurried to get out of the way."

"I hate your guts!"

"Wish we could take you," I say. "I'll send you some post cards."

"Don't bother!" Shacoo says playfully.

Even Rhymin' Sally expresses her disappointment.

> *I don't know why I can't go*
> *I love the ocean, too, you know.*
> *Even though I'm only five*
> *I can sail, swim and even dive.*
> *Mommy and Daddy taught me the Morse Code*
> *And I always do as I'm told.*
> *I could help with the chores*
> *And even man the oars.*

With me aboard
You won't be bored.

"Quite a speech," I say to Sally. Sally's parents own the apple orchard where our clubhouse stands. Our clubhouse is a renovated bunkhouse.

"Quite a reach," Tank whispers in my ear and jabs me in the ribs.

"Don't make fun of Sally," I whisper back, "You're just jealous because you can't speak in rhymes."

Besides the four of us there are twenty other members in the *R*U*1*2s*—no two of us are alike. Our diversity is what makes our club unique. One thing we have in common is our commitment to community service and helping those in need. The only one with an attitude is Cupcake, who keeps us on our toes.

"You look melancholy," Shacoo says.

"I dread being gone so long," I respond.

"You'll be back before you know it."

~~~~~~

THIS IS ONLY THE third time I've flown in an airplane. The first was when I flew to Florida to visit my grandparents when my grandmother had her first operation. The second was when we flew to Anaheim to visit Disney Land to celebrate my tenth birthday. That was two years ago. Tank had never been on an airplane before. His apprehension disappeared once he got in the air. Tank and I sat across the aisle from my parents and Tank had the window seat. I'm not sure how much he captured on his cellphone but he took an awful lot of photographs.

"Can you imagine what Earth looks like from outer space?" Tank asks obviously dazzled by the panoramic view of so much real estate.

"Like what the sun and the moon look like to us I'd rather imagine," I say. "Depending on how far away you are they may appear as only specks."

"Much like the stars."

"Exactly."

Tank is not the only one who shakes his head in wonder and not the only one who has talked about being an astronaut. Both of us have been interested in our vast universe and whether there is life on other planets.

WE'RE MET BY UNCLE Darrell at the San Diego International Airport. It took longer to retrieve our baggage than it took to go from the airport to Uncle Darrell's home. There we were greeted by my Aunt Lynnette and cousins Blake and Brandon. Blake and Brandon are fourteen years old and identical twins. They will be starting high school in the fall. Both are great athletes and love the outdoors. They spend a lot of time skiing in Colorado.

We were barely unpacked before we were down on the beach letting the waves of the Pacific lick our feet. Uncle Darrell showed us through *The Last Harrah*, the replacement for *The Bailey Four*. Even my parents were impressed by Uncle Darrell's new yacht. It wasn't just the size but the craftsmanship that made us stand there with our mouths wide open. "Had to build a new slip to moor our new yacht," Uncle Darrell says. "It's almost twice the size of the old one."

"Thought we'd take an overnighter out onto the Pacific while you're here," Uncle Darrell says to Dad. "Know a fishing spot where you can catch a trophy swordfish or Marlin."

"Suits me," Dad says. "I need something to hang on the wall at the clinic."

"What about us?" I ask.

"And the four of you, too," Uncle Darrell responds as he looks at Tank and me and his two sons.

I look at Tank. He raises his eyebrows and nods.

"I'm not sure my parents would like a stuffed swordfish or Marlin hanging on our living room wall," Tank says.

"We can hang them on the wall at the R*U*1*2s' clubhouse," I suggest. "The place could use a little sprucing up."

"Isn't it a little premature to be discussing where you're going to put your trophy?" Dad asks. "You've got to find, snag and reel one in before you try to figure out where it's going."

~~~~~~

I LAY AWAKE PICTURING myself standing on the docks at Fiddler's Cove Marina with my swordfish on a scale and everyone gathered around admiring my catch. I can also picture the headlines in the daily newspaper: *TWELVE YEAR OLD SETS WORLD RECORD WITH RECORD CATCH*. I'm brought back to reality when I remember what Dad said: "You've got to find, snag and reel one in before you try to figure out where it's going." I'm also reminded by what my grandpa always says: "Don't count your chickens before they hatch." I fall asleep thinking of our day on the sea.

~~~~~~

BOTH DAD AND UNCLE Darrell are disappointed when Mom and Aunt Lynnette decline to accompany us on our day's excursion aboard *The Last Harrah*. "Opportunity only knocks once!" Dad says to Mom.

"Are you talking about a bumpy ride on the Pacific or me going shopping with Lynnette?" Mom replies. "The Pacific doesn't look all that inviting today."

"We wouldn't want you gals to spoil your fun by not spending money or mussing your hair," Uncle Darrell teases.

"We'd only be in the way," Aunt Lynnette says. "Besides coming home wind chafed, sunburned, cold, tired and wet somehow doesn't appeal to us ladies—does it Olivia?"

"Not if they want dinner waiting for them when they return," Mom replies and smiles.

And so our journey begins without Mom and Aunt Lynnette.

CHAPTER TWO

A HOSTILE SEA

Being in a boat without a paddle" was something my other grandfather used to say. It was not something I fully understood until after several hours into our journey and the sea turned into a nightmare. The skies blackened and we were surrounded by water on all sides. The torrent of rain pelted down on us and the swells from below created by a hostile wind crashed against *The Last Hurrah* as if it *were* the last hurrah.

"I've never seen it like this!" Uncle Darrell says as we all hang on for dear life.

"Maybe we should head closer to shore," Dad says. "Or maybe even back to port."

Uncle Darrell attempts to do as Dad suggests, having been in the Navy and all.

It is not long before Uncle Darrell steers the boat inadvertently into an outcropping of rock damaging the rudder.

"We're heading in the wrong direction!" Dad tells Uncle Darrell.

"Can't help it," Uncle Darrell says. "Our rudder is disabled and it's now nature that is governing our course."

This is exciting stuff for Tank and me. That is until the yacht starts taking on water.

"It appears the bilge keel has been damaged," Uncle Darrell says, "and maybe even the bilge itself. I'll start the pumps since water is starting to seep in."

"What a way to start a vacation!" I say to Tank.

Tank doesn't say anything. He's shaking like a leaf.

"Shouldn't you turn off the engine and flip the fuel shutoff valve?" Dad asks Uncle Darrell.

"Good idea," Uncle Darrell replies. "We're not going anywhere anyway."

When Uncle Darrell returns he tries the two-way radio. When it doesn't work he says, "Must be shorted out. Unfortunately I'm not as familiar with the new rig as I was with the old one. Did anyone remember to bring a cellphone?"

"Dad told us to leave our valuables and everything we didn't want to get damaged or wet in our rooms," I say.

"Turned out to be bad advice," Dad says. "I left mine behind because I didn't want our day to be interrupted by pesky telephone calls. Our partner is fielding our calls while Olivia and I are away."

Neither Blake nor Brandon brought theirs either. So much for wanting an uninterrupted day on the sea. What was it I said about being in a boat without a paddle?

THE SEA IS A little calmer as we drift on the Pacific. Fortunately plenty of drinking water and food staples are stored in waterproof barrels. And what Aunt Lynnette packed for the day is in a waterproof container.

After being afloat for about six hours we find ourselves drifting into a quiet cove of a fairly large island. Dad jumps out and tethers the yacht to a tree. Soon we are all on land off the hostile sea. I watch as the yacht jostles about on the wake and wonder how long we'll be stranded.

"Hey you castaways, anybody hungry?" Uncle Darrell asks. When he gets the answer he no doubt was waiting for he goes out to retrieve our lunch. Brandon goes with him and the two wade back carrying the cooler Aunt Lynnette packed. Uncle Darrell also returns with a map and a compass.

After we scarf down lunch, Dad asks Uncle Darrell, "Where are we and how long do you suppose we'll be stranded?"

"I'm guessing we're here," and Uncle Darrell points to the Los Coronados Islands, a group of islands only twenty miles or so from San Diego. We're in kind of a secluded spot so it's hard telling when the next boat will come our way. In the interim I guess we'll just have to hope and pray."

"That bad?"

"No use fooling ourselves. With four boy scouts and two ex-boy scouts we should be able to survive for quite some time." Uncle Darrell looks at Blake, Brandon, Tank and me and says, "Right boys?"

We all nod.

"Just hope we don't have to rub two sticks together to start a fire," I say. "I was never good at that."

"The matches and a first aid kit are in waterproof containers on *The Last Hurrah*," Uncle Darrell says. "We've not had her for very long but I know where all the safety equipment is located."

"Think we have the wherewithal to repair the yacht and limp her back to port?" Dad asks.

"As I said I'm not as familiar with *The Last Hurrah* as I was with *The Bailey Four*. I was in a hurry to get *The Last Hurrah* and have her operational by the time you arrived and know little about her. Hope that doesn't prove to be a bad mistake."

"Let's go explore the island," Brandon suggests.

"Why don't you four boys go ahead," Uncle Darrell says, "while Jackson and I assess the damage to *The Last Hurrah* and plan a way to get discovered and rescued. Be grateful we have an M.D. in our midst."

"Be careful and don't wander off too far," Dad warns, "and watch out for wild animals. Who knows what is lurking out there."

"I have the compass," Blake says and pulls it from his pocket.

We don't get very far down a fairly well-defined path before we spot what we think are footprints of a bear. We fashion some tree limbs, thanks to the Boy Scout knives Tank and I are packing, into spears.

"Probably won't be very effective," Tank says.

"Better than nothing," I respond.

Blake and Brandon don't seem to be all that concerned. However when they scare out some wild turkeys along the path they both jump and hold their spears in a defensive manner. *So much for bravery*. At least Tank and I remain calm.

Along the path we notice there are a lot of wild berries growing. I recognize the raspberries and blackberries, Tank the choke cherries. Not far off the path are several mulberry bushes. We sample the raspberries and blackberries. They taste surprisingly sweet.

When we catch up to Blake and Brandon they relate they had scared up several deer and some rabbits.

"At least we're not going to go hungry," I tell Tank.

"Now just how do you think we're going to bag them?" Tanks asks.

"We have several guns in the hold of the yacht," Brandon says. "The shells are in a waterproof ammo container."

As we walk some distance down the path we hear the sounds of drums in the distance. As we draw near we hear the chant, "Ooh, wah—wah; ooh, wah—wah," and we see natives in bright beaded outfits, feathered headdresses and moccasins dancing either a rain dance or a war dance. Since there has been more than an abundance of rain we assume it must be a war dance.

We stop in our tracks and find a dense thicket to hide behind just off the beaten path and just in time to avoid being seen by a group of young maidens coming in our direction balancing large clay jugs on their heads. They're engrossed in chatter as they walk down the path in single file and veer off in the direction of the sea.

"We've hit Flamingo Island," Brandon says. "It's a private island inhabited by the descendants of the Quechuan Indian tribe. I recognize the warriors' headgear."

"They are very territorial," Blake says. "I'm surprised *The Last Hurrah* was not spotted when we came ashore. Because it's so close to their encampment it's hard to believe we were not noticed."

"Since none dare trespass," Brandon says, "security is no doubt lax. Maybe the noise of the storm and the dark sky distracted them."

"Thank God for that!" Blake says.

"What are you guys saying?" I ask.

"Shhh!" Blake says as several more maidens pass down the path.

After they're a safe distance away, Brandon says, "Flamingo Island is not an island you want to get stranded on. The natives here are fearful they will be dispossessed of what they consider sacred ground and relocated on some type of reservation. Our government has chosen to grant them sanctuary and they are considered a sovereign nation free from outside interference."

"What would happen if we were discovered?" Tank asks.

"That is a well-kept secret," Blake says. "Let's just say that if anyone has been stranded on the island, there's no record of it."

I look at Tank and we both are filled with terror. *We want to be discovered but not by the descendants of the Quechuan Indians!*

"Let's…go back!" Tank suggests. "I don't want to become the poster child of an intruder hung out to dry or shark bait."

When we arrive back at the cove, Uncle Darrell and Dad have a fire blazing and our spare clothes drying on a make-shift clothes line.

"So how are the castaways holding up?" Dad asks.

The four of us excitedly tell him what we've discovered and wait for a reaction.

"Unless you want to swim across the Pacific," Uncle Darrell says, "we have to stay put and hidden until we're spotted and rescued."

"How can we ever be discovered if we stay hidden?" I ask.

"Eventually a passing ship will travel in our direction," Uncle Darrell says. "Then we'll try to make our plight noticed without alerting the other inhabitants of the island."

"It's like walking a tightrope," I say and suddenly find myself growing weary from fatigue and worry.

"Are we going to spend the night aboard *The Last Hurrah?*" Brandon asks Uncle Darrell.

"Best we spend it ashore. The sleeping bags should be dry by bed time. Afraid *The Last Hurrah* is taking on too much water."

"But…" Blake says, "the water in the cove is pretty shallow and the yacht can't sink too much further. Wouldn't we be safer aboard *The Last Hurrah?*"

"We're taking a chance either way. Even if we're aboard *The Last Hurrah* there's no guarantee we won't be spotted by the natives," Uncle Darrell says.

When we tell Dad and Uncle Darrell about what we think was a war dance, Uncle Darrell wades out to *The Last Hurrah* and retrieves two rifles and a canister containing shells. Blake goes with him and returns with a couple of flashlights that were on a shelf in the cabin and out of the water.

After a change of clothes and more of Aunt Lynnette's care package my anxiety subsides a little. Tank is not as uptight as I thought he'd be. The evening air is warm and the sleeping bags become our security blankets. Although I'm tired I have difficulty falling asleep. I jump at every strange sound and struggle to control my imagination.

Dusk seems to be short-lived and soon we are counting the stars and watching the flames from the fire dance in the darkness. My eyelids grow heavy and I'm unable to stay awake any longer. When the morning light awakens me I can hear the tide slap against the shore and rock *The Last Hurrah*. Miraculously the yacht is still afloat and we've not been detected by the natives. *A good sign!* Everyone else is still asleep. I attempt to fall back asleep but can't. I keep thinking of my mother and Aunt Lynnette who must have been worried sick when we had not returned home the night before. *What must they be thinking?*

CHAPTER THREE
THE HOMEFRONT

ad weather doesn't always spell disaster," Lynnette says reassuringly.

"Being late for dinner on top of a squall does," Olivia says and stays by the window.

"Darrell and the boys have survived worse storms. With a new and bigger yacht the odds are in their favor."

"I still can't help but worry. No telling how bad the storm was in the middle of the Pacific."

"The waves are not as menacing as they were," Lynnette says as she, too, peers out the window. "Plus Darrell has a radio system with a range further than they could have travelled in the few hours they have been gone."

"I don't know. They've been gone at least six hours. That's a long time without any word. I checked in the boys' room and Tank's and Genius's cellphones are on the dresser. Same with Jackson's."

"IT'S NOT LIKE DARRELL not to send word if they're going to be delayed. In fact it's highly unusual for him to be gone after dusk. I better call the Coast Guard." Lynnette pulls out an address book and dials a number.

"United States Coast Guard Chief Warrant Officer Brady Hudson speaking."

"Yes, Officer Hudson, this is Lynnette Bailey. I'm worried about my husband and members of our family who I'm afraid have been lost in the storm at sea."

"What was their place of origination and what was their destination?"

"We have a beach home here in Coronado and they left here sometime around 8:45 or 9:00 a.m. in a yacht named *The Last Hurrah*. They went out on the Pacific to do some deep sea fishing."

"That was just prior to the storm. I take it you've had no communication from them since their departure."

"Correct. *The Last Hurrah* is a new vessel we just purchased and a vessel my husband is not all that familiar with."

"How large a craft is *The Last Hurrah?*"

"Thirty-three feet."

"That's more than large enough to have survived the storm. Is there a special location where he fishes?"

"He has a special area where he goes but I can't describe it since there are no landmarks."

"Is it north or south of Coronado Beach?"

"South, I would say."

"We responded to a rescue north of Coronado earlier in the day when a smaller vessel with a different name was blown by the high winds into a rock outcropping damaging its hull. There were some other minor mishaps that we responded to but none to vessels matching the description you have given me and none with the name *The Last Hurrah*."

"I'm sorry I can't give more information. *The Last Hurrah* was equipped with a GPS and a fairly sophisticated radio system. My husband is a former Navy man and his brother who is aboard is a medical doctor. Our two sons and their cousin are boy scouts and have survival training. I assume the fourth boy is a boy scout as well."

"Was *The Last Hurrah* equipped with a life boat or raft and was everyone equipped with life jackets?"

"Yes. My husband being a former Navy man as I mentioned was a stickler when it came to life jackets."

"The Coast Guard has a number of boats patrolling the Pacific particularly near the populated areas. I'll pass on the information you related and get a helicopter in the air pronto. Again I am Chief Warrant Officer Brady Hudson. Let me know if and when they return or otherwise we will continue with our search and rescue efforts."

"Thank you Officer Hudson. And if you find out anything you have my number on your caller I.D."

After Lynnette hangs up Olivia says, "I'd better call Tank's parents and let them know what's going on. I hesitate to alarm them unnecessarily but I know if I were them I would be upset by not being so informed."

"I'm still not in a panic," Aunt Lynnette says. "On the edge maybe. But not over the edge. It's easy for Darrell and the boys to lose track of time—especially when Jackson and Genius are around. But in an unfamiliar boat on a stormy sea is cause for concern. If they don't show or we don't hear from them in the next half hour or so then I'd recommend you call Tank's parents."

"BONNIE, THIS IS OLIVIA. We made it to San Diego okay." Olivia hits the speaker button.

"Olivia, you sound distressed. Is…is everything alright?"

"The operative word is worried. Tank and Genius went on a deep sea fishing excursion with Jackson's brother Darrell and his two sons. They're way overdue and Darrell's wife Lynnette and I are pacing the floors."

"Oh, my! Let me put Liam on the extension."

After a brief pause Tank's dad is on the line. "Olivia, Bonnie says Tank is missing at sea along with Genius and Jackson."

"It may be a little premature but our respective sons have not returned from their fishing trip with Genius' uncle and two cousins. We've called the Coast Guard and alerted them. Fortunately Jackson is with them and they are on my brother-in-law's new yacht that is equipped with all the latest safety gadgets."

"It's still early," Liam says. "Hopefully they just let the day slip away from them. I assume the yacht is equipped with lights, a two-way radio and safety equipment."

Lynnette nods as Olivia looks in her direction.

"Yes," Olivia responds. "Our cause for concern is that a sudden unexpected squall occurred earlier in the day. Unfortunately Jackson insisted they all leave their cellphones at home to avoid them getting lost or ruined by the water. However they do have the two-way radio but there's been no communication with *The Last Hurrah* which is unusual according to my sister-in-law."

Liam is silent for a few moments. He then asks, "Are you alarmed enough to have us fly out there?"

Lynnette shakes her head.

"Probably not but I thought you should know."

"Absolutely! Thanks for the heads up. By the way were the boys wearing life jackets or do you know?"

"Yes. We're positive they were because that's one thing my brother-in-law insists on."

"Life boat," Lynnette mouths.

"And the yacht was equipped with a rubber raft," Olivia says. "Perhaps we're seeing ghosts."

"Not at all!" Liam says. "We'll take the next flight out if need be."

"Why don't you wait a while? Lynnette sees no reason to panic at this point. Darrell retired after twenty years in the Navy. I think that's the reason I'm remaining calm. I trust he has the knowledge to cope with any situation that arises at sea. It's possible the craft just became disabled in the squall and they're floating around waiting to be rescued. The Coast Guard has been alerted and they're searching as well. We'll keep you informed step-by-step of whatever we hear. But in the interim don't forget nothing can trump the power of prayer."

CHAPTER FOUR

UNEXPECTED VISITORS

Uncle Darrell wades out to *The Last Hurrah* and brings back some of the emergency food supplies that were stored aboard. Soon we're drinking powdered orange juice and eating cereal with chunks of dried fruit soaked in powdered milk. There wasn't much left of the lunch Aunt Lynnette packed the day before other than some apples, cookies and chips. But food is food. It's better than baked frogs, snails or worms.

The sun has warmed the day and my cousins, Tank and I retrieve the swim suits we brought. As we frolic in the shallow waters of the cove while Uncle Darrell and Dad fuss with the two-way radio we spot the sails of a ship on the horizon. It looks like it's coming our direction but appears to be travelling at a snail's pace.

"There's a ship out there!" I yell at Dad. We're immediately in a frenzy trying to figure out how to attract the ship's attention without causing a stir on the island.

"Don't want to alert the natives if we can avoid it," Uncle Darrell warns.

The fire from the night before still has some live embers. Tank shouts, "Pile evergreen branches on the fire and the smoke will signal we're here."

"Great idea!" I say.

Everyone scurries to fill the sky with smoke. Brandon is the only one with an axe. He brought it ashore the night before just in case there was a wild animal lurking about. Brandon does the hacking and we do the stacking as Rhymin' Sally would say.

As the ship draws closer Uncle Darrell identifies it as a clipper ship.

Looking out to sea and shielding his eyes with his hands, Uncle Darrell says, "It's definitely not a recreational vessel! Carrying too much cargo."

We all run up and down the shore waiving and shouting. When the ship gets close enough for us to make out details we notice it's flying a Jolly Roger flag. Holy Moly! A pirate ship!

We all stop in our tracks, "What do we do now?" I ask.

"Genius," Dad says, "I'm afraid it's too late to do anything. There's no place to hide and we can't outrun them."

"Don't panic! Just let me see what they want," Uncle Darrell says. "Maybe we can negotiate with them. I've had a lot of practice negotiating in my work."

"Good suggestion, Darrell. Let's hope they speak our language," Dad says.

"Don't count on it!" Uncle Darrell says as we watch the pirate ship inch closer and closer.

~~~~~~~

I'M NOT AS FRIGHTENED as I thought I'd be when the pirate ship stops before it hits shallow waters. The pirates lower a small boat and row in our direction. If I didn't know better I would have thought this bunch was fresh from a Hollywood movie set. It was obvious they were not wearing costumes; they were dressed in what must have been, from the looks of them, their regular clothes. At least Hollywood got it right by mimicking actual pirate apparel—not the other way around.

When the crew gets out of the boat they don't appear to be menacing. Although they are carrying rifles they don't point them directly at us. We later learn that the one who appears to be the leader is nicknamed Patch. And for good cause. He has a black patch over his left eye—just like in the movies.

Patch speaks in a language none of us understand. Tank and I would later refer to it as "pirate speak."

Uncle Darrell steps up, "We're from the U.S.A.," he says as the pirates approach.

"Ach! U.S.A.," Patch says. "I don' talk English." He then motions for one of the other pirates to come forward.

"I'm Bad Bart," the newcomer says in a husky voice, "from Brooklyn. What youse guys doing on this island?"

Uncle Darrell continues to be the spokesperson for us. He says, "We're shipwrecked. Our yacht was badly damaged in the storm and we were washed ashore."

We watch Bad Bart translate for Patch. After a brief conversation between the two Bad Bart says, "Patch likes your skiff. Thinks we can repair it with the parts we have on board the *Marauder.*"

"That would be great!" Uncle Darrell says.

"Doesn't sound much like they're planning to give it back once it's repaired," Dad says to Uncle Darrell.

"What was that?" Bad Bart asks.

"Hope you have the parts," Dad responds.

Tank and I just look at each other hoping Dad's comment to Uncle Darrell doesn't spark some kind of adverse reaction.

More conversation between Bad Bart and Patch after which Bad Bart says, "Hawk and Gore are going back to the *Marauder* to see what parts we have in stock. First they want to inspect the damage to your rig. Doesn't look like she's sea worthy and can be towed."

Hawk and Gore are already examining *The Last Hurrah*. They look her over from stem to stern.

Apparently trying to be helpful Uncle Darrell says, "Has a hole in the bilge and the rudder was damaged when we ran her against some rocks."

Bad Bart nods and goes over and speaks to Hawk and Gore again in pirate speak. After a brief conversation, he comes back and reports to Patch. I notice the other pirates are keeping us under careful watch. Hawk, Gore and Bad Bart repeat the process several more times before Bad Bart returns to where we're standing.

"We've a repair kit on the *Marauder* and can patch 'er—at least well enough to tow 'er," Bad Bart says. "Then we'll pull 'er out of the shallows and take 'er as close to the *Marauder* as we can and hook 'er up." Looking back over his shoulder toward Patch, Bad Bart says, "Patch says for doing that and the repair he's gonna keep 'er in payment."

"But—," Uncle Darrel begins to protest.

"Don't think you understand," Bad Bart says. "You don't have a choice in the matter. We can either take you and the yacht with us and guarantee you safe passage or take the yacht and leave you here to fend for yourselves and hope the elements, wild animals and natives don't get you before you starve to death."

That little speech gets our attention. Tank looks at me and we both cringe. I look at Dad and he shrugs.

"It's up to Darrell," Dad says. "It's his yacht. However doesn't look like it matters much what he thinks. The pirates are going to take *The Last Hurrah* regardless. I would opt for the sure thing."

Uncle Darrell looks at Dad and says, "We can't risk the lives of the four boys. If it comes to forfeiting *The Last Hurrah* for safe passage home I also opt for the sure thing."

"We'll go with you," Darrell tells Bad Bart. "Is it possible once we're aboard the *Marauder* we can radio our families in San Diego and let them know that we're safe and for them not to worry?"

Bad Bart replies, "Once we're in international waters you can use one of our cellphones. Until we're out of reach of the U.S. authorities you'll be restricted from any outside contact. In fact I'll need to confiscate your cellphones."

"We left them at home," I blurt.

A broad smile crosses Bad Bart's face and I notice he even has the typical gold tooth. "Wise decision lad," he says.

I can't make up my mind whether I like Bad Bart or not. Everything I've read about pirates has been negative.

"What do you think?" I whisper to Tank.

"Not sure what the *R*U*1*2s* will think when we tell them about spending part of our summer vacation with pirates," Tank says.

"They'll think we made the whole thing up."

Once the six of us are aboard the *Marauder* we're shown our quarters. They are surprisingly clean and roomy. When we boarded the pirate ship the other pirates stared at us as if we were Martians and from another planet.

When we boarded Dad noticed one of the pirates had a blood soaked bandage on his hand.

"What happened fellow?" he asked.

Bad Bart translated for Patch and Patch nodded his head giving permission.

"Sea Dog was injured when a heavy barrel slipped and crushed his hand."

"I'd like to take a look at it," Dad says, "I'm a doctor."

When they find out Dad is a medical doctor he's immediately whisked away to the sickbay area of the ship where a number of patients along with Sea Dog receive immediate attention. Later Dad would say, "You would think it was a hospital ship with all the drugs and medical supplies they had on hand."

Blake, Brendon, Tank and I are soon handed buckets of soapy water and mops and told to swab the deck. I whisper to Tank, "Some vacation this turned out to be."

"You'll be treated no different than anyone else," Bad Bart says as he leads us topside. Uncle Darrell is taken into the control room and instructed to service the computers. Apparently the pirates had the equipment— just didn't know how to install it.

By now *The Last Hurrah* has been repaired and is attached to the back of the *Marauder*. The water has been pumped from the bilge and it is now sea worthy. Being towed we can't tell whether it could operate on its own. "Don't think they were able to fix the rudder," Uncle Darrell says. "Without a rudder it's useless."

Looking back at the camp near where *The Last Hurrah* was moored we see a group of natives milling around scrounging through the debris.

"They must have seen our smoke signal," Tank says.

"Good thing they didn't see it sooner," I reply.

"Good thing the pirates didn't waste any time in getting *The Last Hurrah* patched up and out of gunshot range," Uncle Darrell says. "They'd be no match for us!" Bad Bart says apparently listening to our discussion. "The natives usually run when we're anywhere near their island. And we spent the night anchored at the far end of the island. That may be why you weren't their breakfast."

CHAPTER FIVE
SHIP AHOY

We're in the mess hall just finishing lunch when Bad Bart hands Dad and Uncle Darrell each a cellphone. "Patch says it's okay to call your families and let them know you've been picked up by a 'cruise ship!'"

"Thank you very much," Dad says as he accepts the phone. "We know they're probably worried sick." Dad gestures for me to join him before he dials Mom's phone number.

When I make my way across the deck to join Dad I hear Tank ask Bad Bart, "Do you have a spare? I'd like to call *my* parents."

"You mean you're not...?" Bad Bart squints and points at me. "You two are not brothers?"

"No," Tank says. "We're like brothers... kinda like you and your, your, ah, your sailor friends here."

Bad Bart nods and leaves. From where I'm huddled with Dad, I watch him return and hand Tank a third cellphone.

"Here, use this," he says.

In the interim I see Blake and Brandon huddle with Uncle Darrell. Dad punches in Mom's number and hits the speaker button.

After one ring, Mom answers, "Hello." I can tell she's been crying.

"Olivia, it's me Jackson. Genius is here beside me."

"Oh, thank God!" Mom exclaims. Then after a pause she asks, "Are you two all right? I…I…we've been worried sick…" I can hear her sobbing.

"It's okay, Olivia, we're okay!" Dad reassures her. "No need to worry. We were shipwrecked during the storm and became stranded on an island. We spent the night there."

"Shipwrecked! Oh, my! Did the boat sink?"

"No, but it was severely damaged."

"Genius!" Mom blurts.

"I'm right here, Mom, Dad has you on speaker."

"Thank God you're alright," Mom says. "And the others?"

"They're alright too. Darrell, Blake and Brandon are in the midst of calling Lynnette."

"What about Tank?"

"He's fine. He's calling his parents as we speak."

"That's good. I spoke to Bonnie and Liam…by the way where are you and where did you get the phone?"

"Oh, ah, we're on a cruise ship," Dad says and cringes when he looks at me.

"A cruise ship? Why didn't you call sooner? We've all been on pins and needles! I've worn out my knees praying."

"I know, Olivia, but we didn't have a chance to call sooner. The two-way radio on Darrell's yacht was damaged during the storm and this is the first real opportunity we've had to call. None of us brought our cellphone with us when we left as you probably already know and we're now using borrowed phones."

"I did notice you left without your cellphones and that troubled me. By the way what's the name of the cruise ship that picked you up?"

"Ah, it's called *Marauder.*"

"*Marauder* ? Never heard of it! What cruise line?"

"Well it's more like a *private cruise ship*," Dad says. "They don't advertise."

Bad Bart smiles as he listens to the conversation. His name is certainly deceiving. I'm not sure I want to know how he got it but as far as the six of us are concerned it's nothing more than just a nickname.

"I miss you and Genius," Mom says. "Where are you and when are you coming home?"

"I'm not sure where we are. The ship can't change course just to accommodate us. Looks like we'll have to wait until it reaches its destination. And then I'm not sure it's coming back this way again."

"And where will that be and how long will that take?" Mom asks anxiously.

"Hopefully not in China. Don't know what the timeframe is. We'll call you when we get there." Dad looks at Bad Bart and he nods.

"Okay, but please call us as often as you can," Mom pleads. "And get back here as soon as you can!"

After we exchange the "I love yous" and hang up, I ask Bad Bart if I can use the cellphone to call a friend to let her know what's happening.

"Friend, huh! Who's this friend?"

"Her name is Shacoo and she's my age."

Bad Bart playfully punches my bicep. "Aren't you a little young to have a girlfriend?"

"She's…ah, …a classmate and a member of the R*U*1*2s—a club she, Tank and I helped form with nineteen other friends and school chums."

"Okay, you can call. Just be careful what you say. You know her number?"

"Have it memorized."

Bad Bart hands me the phone and I jab in Shacoo's number. Shacoo's mother answers. "Bandaris' residence."

"Mrs. Bandaris, this is Genius. Is Shacoo there?"

"Genius! Didn't recognize the telephone number. How's the vacation going?" she asks.

"Oh, you know, sailing the ocean blue," I say hoping she won't press for details. "I'm using a borrowed cellphone."

"Hang on," she says and I hear her shout Shacoo's name.

Moments later Shacoo is on the phone. "Genius, what a pleasant surprise."

"Hey, Shacoo." I'm happy to hear her voice.

"Where are you calling from?"

I look out at the ocean. There's no land in sight. "Oh, somewhere on the Pacific. Not sure exactly."

"Good thing you're not navigating the vessel. No telling where you'd end up."

"Ha, ha. That's really funny," I say hoping to sound sarcastic and not desperate.

"Didn't expect to hear from you until you and Tank got home. Is everything okay?"

"Why do you ask?"

"Oh, it's just that you sound a little harried. What are you doing in the middle of the Pacific?"

I sigh and say, "We were deep sea fishing and having a great time, that is until we were caught in a bad storm. Uncle Darrell called it a sudden squall and his new yacht, *The Last Hurrah*, was damaged when we sideswiped a rock outcropping. Although the craft was damaged, we didn't sink; we drifted to a deserted island where we spent the night. This morning we were rescued by a passing boat. That's where we are now, on the rescue ship."

"That's really amazing. You won't believe this but I had a funny dream just last night. I dreamed you and Tank were castaways trying to survive on a desolate island."

"That's exactly what happened," I say and collapse to a sitting position on the deck.

Shacoo continues, "The strange part of the dream was that you and Tank had been captured by a band of marauding pirates as you sought to be rescued. It was pretty scary."

"Yep, that is strange," I say. "How did your dream end?"

"With Mom waking me up for breakfast."

I was glad I hadn't pressed the speaker button. Didn't want Bad Bart to think I said something I shouldn't have. I didn't mention that the name of our rescue ship was the *Marauder*. That was a word or part of a word Shacoo used.

"You have quite an imagination," is all I can manage to say.

When Bad Bart motions for all the cellphones to be returned, I say to Shacoo, "Have to run now. Will call again soon." I hang up wondering if Shacoo was intuitive or that her dream was just an uncanny coincidence.

When Bad Bart moves away Dad whispers to me, "Your mother was relieved. She didn't suspect anything was amiss. She's anxious to have us back and the sooner the better." He then looks toward Uncle Darrell. "I hope his explanation to Aunt Lynnette coincides with ours. Don't want either to worry unnecessarily."

I'M NOT SURE WHAT the future will bring. Strangely I'm not trauma-tized and in fact becoming more intrigued by the minute. These pirates are a finely tuned bunch who remind me of a beehive with all of them buzzing around bent on a single mission. Each seems to know what to do without being told and without get-ting in each other's way. They pay little attention to us as they go about their tasks.

Other than the hum of the *Marauder's* engines and the sound of the waves slapping against the ship everything is peace-ful. That was short lived when everything seemed to turn black and the skies opened up with a downpour reminiscent of the day we were caught in the middle of the infamous storm that devas-tated our boat and left us stranded. The deck cleared and hatch-es were locked. We soon found ourselves in the mess hall playing the pirate's favorite card game *Finagle*. It didn't take long to fig-ure out we made more friends by losing than winning.

After several hours everyone heads topside as the skies clear and the sun lights up the vast expanse of ocean. It's then that the sails of a large ship are spotted on the horizon and coming in our direction. Soon our ship's horns are blaring and the pub-lic announcement system booming in pirate speak, "All hands on deck...all hands on deck...enemy vessel approaching...re-peat enemy vessel approaching!"

The deck is soon swarming with pirates armed with rifles. "What! No sabers?" I flippantly say to Tank.

Tank jabs me in the side with his elbow. "Not the time or place to be clever," he says. "From the looks of things we may wish we had a weapon of our own."

"Find cover," Bad Bart barks at Blake, Brandon, Tank and me. "The *Scourge of the Sea* is heading our way and they're our competition in this section of the Pacific. They're anything but friendly. In return for safe passage we will no doubt have to buy our way out. They usually want food or ammunition."

The four of us jump into a life boat suspended by a rope just above the deck and peer out from under the canvas cover as the *Scourge of the Sea* comes into view. Like the *Marauder* it sports the Jolly Roger flag. The *Scourge of the Sea* looks a lot like the large ships I've seen in our history books. As it gets closer I can see canons trained on us. A band of armed pirates is standing at the rail looking like the ones depicted in one of our text books. Tank and I hunker down under the canvas cover to avoid detection. We peek out occasionally. "They look like they're just itching to engage our crew," I say to Tank.

Out of the group steps a grizzled-looking man who could pass for an NFL defensive lineman or professional wrestler. "Ship ahoy!" he shouts through a megaphone in a raspy voice.

"Ship ahoy!" Patch, who has positioned himself nearest the railing facing the *Scourge of the Sea*, shouts through a megaphone of his own.

The tone of both seems friendly enough. Their pirate speak is still something I don't understand. Maybe it's best I don't.

Blake, Brendon, Tank and I crawl toward one edge of the small life boat to catch a glimpse of what is going on and eavesdrop on the conversation since some of the pirate speak is interspersed with English. In doing so the life boat capsizes and the four of us tumble onto the deck. The clatter catches the attention of the pirates aboard the *Scourge of the Sea* by surprise and they raise their rifles and take aim.

What Patch says at that moment I can't interpret but shortly thereafter Grizz signals his ruffians and barks a command. They lower their weapons. After the discussion turns into a heated argument Patch motions for Bad Bart to step forward. The two talk for a few moments and then Bad Bart motions for the four of us to step forward. As we head in his direction I tell Tank, "Looks like we're the bargaining chips for a safe passage." Tank, who now is shaking like a leaf in a gusty wind, says nothing. I suspect he wishes he hadn't taken me up on the offer to come to California. Even I'm having second thoughts.

"They want two of you to be cabin boys and the other two to handle menial chores at their home base at Crossbones Island," Bad Bart says to Blake, Brandon, Tank and me.

Fearful we may be headed for the China Sea, I ask, "How far is that from here?"

"Does it matter?" Tank says under his breath.

"About 350 nautical miles east of here," Bad Bart responds and points in an easterly direction.

"Can you bargain with them to take just Tank and me," I say.

"You want us to be the martyrs?" Tank asks under his breath.

"You and I are the only two who won't wilt on the vine," I say. "Blake and Brandon are the china dolls in the family. If Grizz and his ruffians will settle for two instead of four why not let them go. Either way it will be the two of us anyway."

"Good point," Tank says and shrinks.

Overhearing our conversation, Bad Bart says, "Let me see if we can't haggle a little. We can offer a cask of wine in the place of Blake and Brandon."

Bad Bart convinces Patch to "negotiate." After a brief discussion with Grizz, whose name we later learn is Gore, a deal is struck. Tank and me together with a cask of wine are exchanged for safe passage of the *Marauder*. I'm grateful that Dad and Uncle Darrell are preoccupied below deck. No telling what chaos they would cause especially if Grizz discovered Dad was a medical doctor.

DAD IS AGAINST TANK and me being whisked away to parts unknown but realizing we have no choice in the matter reluctantly relents. There are tears in his eyes when he
is told by Bad Bart that Tank and I had given up our freedom in exchange for the freedom of Blake and Brandon.
"That's a very noble thing for the two of you to do, Genius,"
Dad says. "To give up your freedom for Blake and Brandon is
something few would do."

"Not really, Dad," I say. "Tank and I would have been forced
to go either way. Besides, Tank and I are survivors and can fi-
nesse our way through this whereas Blake and Brandon might
find it difficult to do so."

"Well, you and Tank are not going alone," Dad says, "I'm
going with you. Better yet I'm going in your place."

"But—"

"No buts about it!"

"Hey, hurry you two," Bad Bart says. "Gore is growing im-
patient."

"I'm going in the boys' place," Dad says to Bad Bart.

Bad Bart gets a quizzical look on his face. "Not sure Gore
will agree but we can ask."

We watch as Bad Bart speaks with Patch. The two argue
before Patch picks up the megaphone and speaks with Gore.
When Bad Bart returns, he says, "I have good news and bad
news. The good news is that Gore is willing—in fact more than
willing when he found out you were a doctor—to take you in
exchange for free passage. The bad news is that he still wants the
two boys."

WHEN WE FIND OUT Gore's crew is headed for the Hawaiian Islands we're elated. "Better than some deserted isle in the Pacific," Dad says.

Dad's medical background comes in handy once again and he's treated as royalty as are Tank and me. As with Bad Bart, Gore has several cellphones at his disposal. He allows us to use one of them to call Mom and Tank's parents.

"You're headed where?" Mom asks.

"Hawaiian Islands," Dad replies.

Long silence. "Can't they drop the six of you off at a closer port?"

"Just Genius, Tank and I are headed for the Hawaiian Islands. Darrell and his two boys will be dropped off probably sooner. I'm not sure of their destination. It's a long story. Genius, Tank and I are on a different 'connecting flight.' Don't fret. We're doing fine. You might want to return to Jefferson City and keep our practice going."

"Oh, sure. You're going to Hawaii and I'm going back to work! Jackson this is all so bizarre. Let me speak to Genius."

"Hi, Mom. We have you on speaker. We're still in the middle of the Pacific. It's not as if we're close to a lot of ports. As Dad says 'beggars can't be choosers.' We're not in any kind of bargaining position and are making the best out of a bad situation."

"You're no longer on the *Marauder*?"

"Ah, no. We're on a different vessel called the *Scourge of the Sea*. She's a clipper ship, only larger than the *Marauder*."

"Good grief, Genius, *Marauder* and *Scourge of the Sea* sound more like pirate ships than cruise ships," Mom says and sighs.

"An experience of a lifetime," I say.

"Darrell will fill you in," Dad says.

"Is Tank okay?"

"As soon as we finish our conversation, he'll call his parents. He doesn't want them to worry either."

"That's what parents do!" Mom says.

"What's that?" I ask.

"Worry!" she responds. "Hopefully, I won't have to do that much longer."

CHAPTER SIX
CHANGING COURSE

When the *Marauder* develops engine trouble and the winds reverse directions Patch decides to change course and replace the Jolly Roger flag with the Stars and Stripes and head back in the direction of San Diego. He also changes his mind about confiscating *The Last Harrah*.

"Patch has decided to reverse course and head back toward San Diego," Bad Bart tells Darrell.

"Does that mean he'll be releasing my two sons and me?" Uncle Darrell asks.

"Yes. He also needs to find a port where he can repair the engine of the *Marauder* as well as some of the sails that have taken a beating in the recent storms. Apparently impressed by the attitude of you, your brother and the four boys, Patch has had a change of heart. The three of you will be released as soon as we dock."

"We appreciate that. Right now we have a wife and mother who is worrying herself sick over us."

"When your brother nursed Patch back to health, Patch witnessed firsthand that, even in dire circumstances, good men do good deeds. It was then he decided to change and engage in legitimate business ventures and forget the plundering ways of a pirate. He also wants to make amends for having traded his doctor, Genius and Tank to our arch enemy, *The Terrible Dozen.*"

"*The Terrible Dozen?*" Darrell asks.

"Yep! That's what the crew of the *Scourge* call themselves. They started out with a dozen members. Now they must have close to fifty." Bad Bart hands Darrell a cellphone. "Here call you wife. Tell her we're about two days out and you will call her when we figure out what port we'll be docking at."

"Hello?" Lynnette answers.

"Lynnette!"

"Darrell…"

"Yes, it's me. I'm here with Blake and Brandon."

"Hi, Mom," both boys shout at the same time.

"Thank God! Are you alright?" Lynnette asks and her voice quakes.

"Yes, Lynnette, we're all okay. A little weather beaten but physically we're alright. We have good news and bad news," Darrell says.

"Oh, no!" Lynnette cries into the phone. "Tell me the good news first."

"We're headed back to San Diego towing *The Last Harrah* into port."

"What's the bad news?"

"It'll take the better part of two days."

After a slight pause, Lynnette asks, "How is it the three of you are headed back to San Diego and Jackson, Genius and Tank are headed for Hawaii?"

"Long story that will have to wait until we arrive back home."

<p style="text-align:center">~~~~~~</p>

PATCH MAKES GOOD HIS promise and Uncle Darrell, Blake and Brandon are back home along with their crippled yacht. Lynnette, accompanied by my mother, greets them upon their arrival. According to Mom it was a joyful but emotional reunion. Although their clothes were dirty, tattered and torn and Uncle Darrell had grown a shaggy beard during their time at sea, the only thing that was really "worse for wear," apparently was *The Last Harrah* and that was because of Mother Nature.

We later learned Uncle Darrell helped Patch find someone to repair the *Marauder* and elicited Patch's promise to rescue us from the *Scourge of the Sea* pirates once we reached Hawaii. He also promised to return *The Last Harrah* back over to Uncle Darrell.

CHAPTER SEVEN

THE PLOT THICKENS

Being cabin boys on a pirate ship, especially one the size of the *Scourge of the Sea*, proves to be a challenging task for both Tank and me. In our haste to please everybody we seem to please nobody. Gore runs the clipper ship with an iron-fist. It's not just Tank and me who are fearful of Gore's brutality but his crew as well. His first mate and the counterpart of Bad Bart is a ruffian by the name of Thane. He is every bit as gruff as Gore but unlike Gore he speaks perfect English. All of Gore's orders are funneled through Thane.

The first day is the worst. Both Tank and I believe Gore is laying it on heavy just to see if we can survive. It's a real challenge and both Tank and I are determined we can take all that he dishes out. Part of the stress the first day is to learn pirate jargon and the names for the items Gore is summoning us to fetch. Another is to find out where everything is stored. Fortunately we're not experiencing the sea sickness we experienced on the *Marauder*. And Dad being a medical doctor is right there when we need him.

Dad is preoccupied with several of the pirates who are in sickbay. He has become an instant celebrity much like he had been when we arrived on the *Marauder.* He soon becomes an indispensable member of the crew and is affectionately known as Señor Medico. Like the *Marauder* there is an abundance of medical supplies and prescription drugs aboard. Even Gore spends a day in sickbay with the 24 hour flu bug.

On the way down the coast of Baja California and Mexico the pirates do what pirates do and load the hull of the *Scourge of the Sea* with booty they plunder from ships cruising off shore.

When we reach Central America we're confronted by a rival pirate ship, the *Ocean Raiders.* That clipper ship is about double the size of the *Scourge* and fires several shots across our bow.

"Oh boy, a battle—a real live battle!" I excitedly say to Tank.

Before Tank can answer Thane orders us below deck. Thane is not in the mood to haggle and we do as we're told. We hide behind some crates and are soon joined by my father.

"There is always someone bigger and tougher than you out there," Dad says. "The *Scourge of the Sea* is no match for the *Ocean Raiders,* just like the *Marauder* was no match for the *Scourge of the Sea.* Let's hope the cargo exacted by the *Ocean Raiders* is freight and not human cargo."

"There's no honor among thieves," Tank comments.

Dad nods. "Let's just hope we're not caught in the middle. No telling where we'd end up. At least with Gore and his crew we don't have to worry about 'walking the plank.'"

Tank shrinks further behind our cover as several pirates come aboard and begin removing a number of crates of booty.

When the pirates complete their task and are not within earshot, Dad says, "There goes the loot Gore worked so hard to collect on his way along the coast. Guess they know how it feels to be on the receiving end.

~~~~~~~~

SEVERAL DAYS INTO OUR journey we reach the Hawaiian Islands.

"Not sure where we are exactly," Dad says. "Your mother and I have been to Hawaii many times but never to this island. This is probably headquarters for the Terrible Twelve."

"Terrible Dozen," I correct.

"Same diff," Dad says.

When we reach the docks on the island we're greeted by the families of the pirates of the *Scourge*. Upon finding out that Dad is a medical doctor he's immediately whisked off to care for the sick. Tank and I are integrated into Thane's family and assigned a bedroom with a bunk bed for Tank and me and a single bed for Dad in a rustic cabin that's a stone's throw from the ocean.

"You're going to have to earn your keep!" Thane says to Tank and me. "Hope you are good at washing dishes and floors and doing yard work."

When Thane shows us around we feel more like guests than drudges.

"We're fairly isolated here," Thane says as we walk past an array of cabins that line the ocean front. "Used to be a resort complete with dining hall and swimming pool"

"But...I thought—"

"That we were a primitive band with primitive tastes?"

"We didn't know what to expect," Tank says. These are the first words Tank has spoken to our abductors. Like me Tank has all but shed the terror that engulfed us when we were first handed over to the Terrible Dozen—not knowing what our fate would be. We're still not sure what awaits us.

"A ball park!" Tank says excitedly and points to a baseball diamond similar to what we have back home.

"A little league park," Thane says. "One of the teams is getting ready to practice. Care to join them?"

"Well…ah! Don't we have work to do?"

"When we are in port we manage to relax a few days. There are a half dozen teams that compete and put on a show for the returning pirates."

A foul ball comes in our direction. Tank catches it on the first hop. "Just like the baseballs we have back in the states," Tank says as he examines it.

"We are in the states, stupid," I say to Tank.

"You know what I mean," Tank says and gives me a disapproving glare.

"Let's see you throw it back," Thane says.

When Tank throws the ball a country mile into the hands of the first baseman we are approached by someone who we surmise is the coach.

Thane interprets for us. "The coach wants you to try out for the team. They're short a few players."

Tank and I look at each other. "Little league baseball was our favorite back home," I say. "Count us in."

Thane and the coach converse in pirate speak and Tank and I soon find ourselves playing for the *Bone Crushers*.

"How come their name is in English?" Tank asks.

"Those were the uniforms that we…a…got from a supply ship," Thane responds. "That's where all our team uniforms came from."

Somehow we were able to communicate with the other players and they with us. During the first practice session I pitched while Tank was the catcher. I pitched a no hitter. During batting practice our teammates gathered around while Tank and

I hit the ball. Tank hit most of his over the centerfield wall. "Bravo" must be a universal language because that seemed to be the chant when we made spectacular plays.

"Your main competition is the *Whirlwinds,*" Thane says as we're told we made the team.

~~~~~~

WITH DAD IN THE bleachers seated next to Thane and his wife Bernadine, Tank and I made our debut in the Pacific Pirate League. It was a beautiful Hawaiian evening. Although the wind was not blowing you could hear and see the waves lick the shore. Both Tank and I were nervous. Beforehand we were told by Thane that if we did well we would be placed on shore duty and Gore would "find" other cabin boys. Also we were told Dad would run the makeshift hospital and not be travelling with the pirates as they made their rounds.

In the blink of an eye Tank and I made our mark in the baseball world. The *Whirlwinds* were all we could handle. Much was due to the errors committed by our infield. But for the errors I would have pitched a shutout. With the score tied in the bottom of the ninth inning Tank hit a home run over the centerfield fence. We won two to one. You'd have thought we won the World Series! We were mobbed by the young and the old and everyone else in between.

"Looks like you have a free pass," Thane says as Tank and I are hoisted on the shoulders of our teammates. "Now all you have to do is teach them English and the American way."

~~~~~~

TANK AND I THOUGHT long and hard about changing the course of those who were destined to follow in their fathers' footsteps and those destined to roam the seas plundering, pillaging and robbing.

"Our teammates are just like us in many ways," I tell Tank. "They crave a life full of promise and down deep want to lead a decent life."

"They're being brainwashed to do just the opposite," Tank replies.

"If we can change the thinking of their fathers we can change them."

"How do we do that?"

"If we can convince them that it takes the same amount of effort to earn a dishonest living—no more or less—as it does an honest living then we have a chance. No longer having to look over their shoulders and jumping at every strange noise they hear because they're afraid of getting busted should be incentive enough. Doing good and feeling good about what they do is something most of them have never experienced. Dad might be someone who can help get the point across."

And so it began. Our quest to teach the budding pirates English and an honorable way of life was underway. At first it was at baseball practice and then later with all the children of the pirates at their makeshift school. Then it was with the pirates and their spouses.

Tank and I soon had the respect of the children; Dad the parents. Summer would soon be over so we had to figure a way to acquaint them with a better way of life and the importance of a good education.

"Why not an All Star team—one that could challenge teams in other parts of Hawaii?" Tank asks. "That way the pirates and their families could see how other people live and maybe be persuaded to trade evil for good and at the same time benefit in the process."

Dad becomes an assistant coach for the All Stars and the team's interpreter. We play in a lot of the smaller cities in Hawaii and gain some valuable experience. Next we take on the big five: Waipahu, Kailva, Hilo, Pearl City and ultimately Honolulu. We're a hit and go undefeated. The exposure opens up a number of opportunities for the pirates and also opens their eyes to a better life style. Soon they disband their operation and disburse to various parts of Hawaii. In the process, Dad, Tank and me are released.

Thane drives us to the airport in Honolulu. "Hope we didn't disrupt your lives too much," he says. We say our goodbyes and board the plane.

On the flight back to Jefferson City, Tank says, "I didn't know you could pitch like that."

"When your life depends on it you can do almost anything," I reply. "And you, I didn't know you could catch and hit like that."

"When your life depends on it," Tank says, "you can do almost anything." We both laugh.

<hr />

MOM AND TANK'S PARENTS meet us at the Jefferson City Airport. We postpone telling them what happened until we reach our respective homes.

"Well?" Mom says and raises her brows. The stern look on her face tells me only the unvarnished truth will satisfy her.

When Dad mentions pirates, Mom gasps, "Remember me mentioning the names of the so-called *cruise ships* sounding like the names of *pirate ships*?" she shakes her head and buries her head in her hands. "Why didn't you level with me?"

"We wanted to but our calls were being monitored and we felt fortunate to be able to use the cellphone at all."

"Mom," I say, "we were instructed not to say anything about pirates only that 'a cruise ship' rescued us. We didn't know how hostile our rescuers were and didn't want to cut off our communications all together."

Mom puts her arms around me. "You brave boy," she says. And to Dad she says, "Jackson, I had no idea the situation was so serious. Forgive me for being so insensitive."

We all cry and hug realizing how fragile life really is and that by the grace of God we're back together again—in one piece.

"You two don't look worse for wear," Mom says. "I guess I said that before. I thank God the three of you were released unharmed. I know Tank's parents are also relieved. They were at wits-end with worry. All's well that ends well. Dinner's getting cold!"

"Is it okay if I call Shacoo before we eat?" I ask.

"Go ahead," Mom says. "She's been calling every day and sometimes twice a day worried about you and Tank."

"Is that really you?" Shacoo asks.

"It's me," I say. "We made it home safe and sound."

"We've all been worried," Shacoo whimpers. "Thought you abandoned ship."

"As a figure of speech we did!"

"Can I stop by after dinner? I want to hear all about your adventure at sea. Sure it's a good one."

Shacoo is all ears as I tell her about our harrowing experience at sea, becoming shipwrecked on a desolate island in the Pacific inhabited by unfriendly natives, being rescued by a band of pirates and Tank and I becoming cabin boys on the *Marauder* and the *Scourge of the Sea,* being attacked by the *Ocean Raiders,* being held prisoners on an island occupied by a den of thieves, playing baseball for the *Bone Crushers*, defeating the *Whirlwinds* and playing on an All Star team in Honolulu.

"You've had a boring summer!" Shacoo says. "Now tell me what you really did."

"You don't believe me?"

"You ought to write a children's novel. You've a great imagination."

"What would I call it?" I say, playing along with her tease.

"*My World of Make-Believe* or maybe *My Month as a Would-Be Pirate*. For a minute there you had me believing it all really happened." Shacoo just shakes her head.

"Okay, Smarty, ask my Dad if you don't believe me," I say and call for Dad.

He has not yet shaven and looks like a castaway when he enters the room. Shacoo looks aghast.

"Is that really you, Dr. Bailey?"

"Hello, Shacoo. You're looking at someone who spent a month at sea with a band of pirates and has yet to shave the reminder."

Shacoo looks at me and again at Dad. "Genius wasn't pulling my leg after all?" she asks Dad.

"As improbable as it seems our trip to California was all we expected—and more. The *R*U*1*2s* were well represented by Genius and Tank. They are the true heroes of our ordeal."

"I guess my dream wasn't a dream after all," Shacoo says and puts her arms around me. "You're Superman, Batman, Captain Marvel, Spider Man, Iron Man, Thor and the Incredible Hulk all rolled up into one.

THE NEXT DAY WHEN Tank and I meet with the *R*U*1*2s* we're swarmed by the concerned and the curious. Just at the mention of the word "pirate" Tank and I have their undivided attention. To say we were celebrities was like saying candy is sweet. It was a label that would follow us the rest of the days of our lives. Ours was a story we'd tell over and over again.

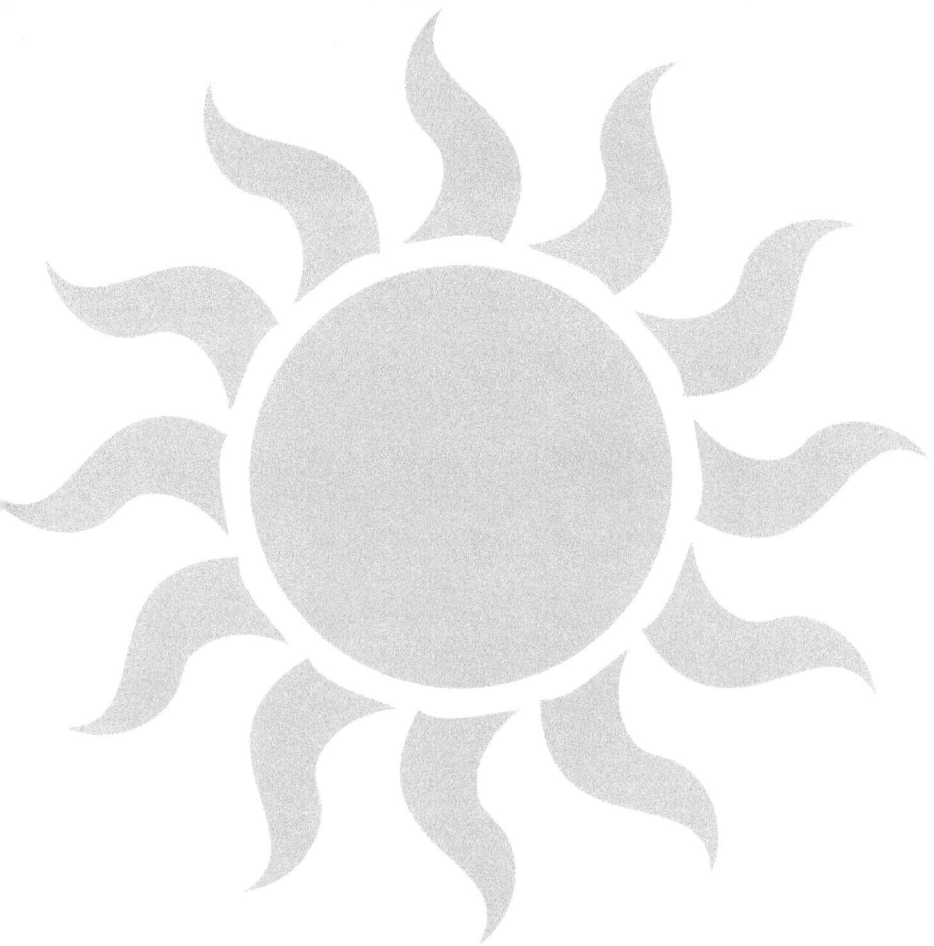

PART TWO
BLAST OFF

CHAPTER EIGHT
TRIP TO OUTER SPACE

Thought you were going to sleep in this morning," Mom says as I stumble into the kitchen rubbing sleep from my eyes and yawning.

"What time is it anyway?" I ask and sit down across from my father who is deeply engrossed in the morning newspaper.

"Did you forget where the kitchen clock is?" Mom asks as she wipes her hands on a dish towel. When the grandfather clock in the dining room chimes eight times I say without looking at the kitchen clock, "It's eight o'clock."

"He doesn't need to look at the clock to tell time," Mom says jokingly to Dad as he looks up from the newspaper.

"He learned that from the pirates earlier this summer," Dad says. "Just by looking at the position of the sun in the sky Genius can tell you what time it is."

"Smart kid we raised," Mom says. "Guess our trip to San Diego wasn't a complete waste of time."

"You're never going to forget are you Olivia?" Dad says and puts his arm around Mom.

"How could I?" she says. "These gray hairs are a constant reminder."

"Anything exciting in the newspaper?" I ask Dad as I reach across the table and pull it toward me.

Mom sets a glass of orange juice in front of me and asks, "Bacon, scrambled eggs and hash browns okay?"

"Better than what we ate aboard the *Marauder* and the *Scourge of the Sea*," I say.

"Anything's better than C rations," Dad says. "Plus we don't have to contend with a table that rocks back and forth with the waves and eat with crews who have no manners."

"I'm heartened the two of you finally quit walking at an angle and holding onto everything for support," Mom says. "Do you still sometimes feel like you're on a boat rocking on turbulent seas?"

"When I'm in bed it sometimes feels like everything is in motion and when I step out onto the floor I expect to be slammed against the wall. Funny what an imagination will do."

"You'll get over it one of these days," Mom says. "Toast or pancakes?"

"Pancakes with lots of melted butter and blueberry syrup."

"Coming right up," Mom says. And to Dad she says, "What is it you didn't want Genius to read in the newspaper?"

"Too late," I say as I glance at the paper and read the front page headlines:

ASTRONAUTS AND AUTHENTIC SPACE CAPSULE TO VISIT JEFFERSON CITY ON TOUR OF USA

"Give me back that newspaper!" Dad snaps jokingly as he pretends to wrestle it away from me. "Genius, haven't you had enough excitement for one summer?"

"Enough excitement to last a lifetime," I say as I excitedly read the front page article.

> *The National Aeronautics and Space Administration (NASA) is conducting its summer tour of the United States with a stop in Jefferson City. 'With an actual space capsule and three astronauts making the visit, it's the closest thing to the real thing,' NASA officials said. 'Set it up right and press the right buttons and you'll soon be in space,' the Jefferson City Gazette was told.*
>
> *The space craft will be set up on an actual launch pad at the Jefferson City fairgrounds and viewing will commence at 8:00 a.m. one week from today. Tickets can be purchased on site for $5.00 for adults and $1.00 for children.*

"Why didn't you want to tell me about this?" I ask Dad. "You know I've always wanted to be an astronaut."

"You didn't give me a chance. Besides, with all the brushes with disaster you faced already this summer, I didn't think you were ready for any more challenges."

"Having survived a tropical storm, a shipwreck, being held captive on two pirate ships and being surrounded by unfriendly natives, I'm ready for almost anything."

"Unfortunately I'm on call next weekend as is your mother. And I'm not sure we want you to go without an adult accompanying you."

"I'd probably be with Tank and Shacoo."

"Okay. But promise you'll all stick together and not do anything stupid."

"I promise."

I COULDN'T WAIT TO get to the *R*U*1*2s'* clubhouse after reading the NASA article. I was eager to share the news with Shacoo and Tank. I think that was because none of the three of us have brothers or sisters and are as close as siblings.

Shacoo is a dedicated student. She has always been at the top of her class. The *R*U*1*2s* revere her. Shacoo's mother's name is Katrina, but she is known as Katie, and Shacoo's father's name is Carlo. He is a biologist employed as a lab technician for Chemical Technology Resources, Inc. here in Jefferson City and does lab work for the police.

You already know about Tank. He is the son of Jefferson City's police chief, Liam O'Malley. Tank is a husky twelve-year old and is probably destined to become a football star though he aspires to be an astronaut. Being the son of the police chief, Tank is privy to the most up to date innovations in the law enforcement community and loves sharing his knowledge with the *R*U*1*2s.* His dad and Shacoo's dad work together solving crimes.

When I arrive at the clubhouse I notice Shacoo and Tank are there ahead of me. I leap from my bike and burst in. Out of breath I ask, "Did you guys see the morning paper?"

Tank is the first to respond. "Yep. Can you believe it?"

"Pretty neat," Shacoo says. "What a way to end our summer vacation."

"It just doesn't get any better than this?" I say. "A rocket ship in our own backyard!"

We're soon joined by the other *R*U*1*2s*. Several are carrying the newspaper account announcing the arrival of the spacecraft. Suddenly everyone is a budding astronaut.

CHAPTER NINE

HOUSTON, WE HAVE A PROBLEM

The day before the expected public viewing of the spaceship the *R*U*1*2s* meet at the clubhouse. Everyone is bubbling over with excitement at the prospect of actually touring an authentic space shuttle.

Scooter, Sonny and Toby enter the clubhouse together. They just completed the fourth grade. The three boys are as close as brothers and we often refer to them as the three little musketeers.

"Yesterday afternoon we rode our bikes down to the fairgrounds and watched as the NASA caravan pulled up and unloaded the shuttle," Scooter says. His voice cracks with excitement.

"Yeah!" Toby squeals. "It was pretty crowded and we didn't get very close but I can tell you it's going to be something to go aboard. I probably won't sleep tonight thinking of tomorrow."

"Speaking of which," Shacoo says. "We need to separate into groups because we can't all go in at the same time. I read in the newspaper that only four people would be allowed in the shuttle at one time. It said the tour would take approximately fifteen minutes per group."

"I saw that, too," Penny says. "How do you suggest we determine who goes with who? Draw straws?"

"Well, I was thinking since we've pretty much established who our BFFs are we just stay in those groups. Anybody have a better idea?" Shacoo asks.

I watch the members look around and pretty soon everyone is nodding—that is all except Rhymin' Sally.

"Sally," I say, but before I can finish my sentence, Sally blurts out,

> *Oh sure, that works for all of you,*
> *Am I the only one with a clue?*
> *Carly hooks up with his friend Rusty*
> *They'll include Tanner and Dusty.*
> *The fifth graders, Candy and Niki*
> *Will probably go in with Willy and Wiki.*
> *That leaves Pudgy and Diego*
> *To link up with Mohawk and Pineapple.*
> *The only ones left are Cupcake and me*
> *And how much fun do you think that'd be?*

At the end of her tirade Sally begins to cry. Cupcake, not to be outdone, stands and stomps her foot in defiance. "Don't worry about me spoiling your fun, Sally. I'm not going to go. I have claustrophobia and mother wouldn't allow it anyway." Cupcake jerks her jacket from the back of her chair and storms out the door slamming it behind her.

A bewildered looking Sally asks Shacoo,

> *Is claustrobia catching like measles or mumps*
> *Where you get all red and covered with bumps?*

"No, it's not contagious. It's the fear of being in closed, tight quarters," Shacoo says.

Oh, I see,

Then that's not me.

"No, it isn't." Shacoo says. She looks at me and then at Tank and we know what's coming. We both reluctantly nod our agreement. Shacoo smiles and says, "Sally, you're going to go in with Genius, Tank and me."

Sally jumps up and grabs Shacoo's hand.

Oh, goodie, goodie, now I see

I'm the fourth in your party of three.

I look at Shacoo and shrug. *Here we go again.* I close my eyes and count to ten.

~~~~~~~

THE DAY WE'VE BEEN waiting for dawns bright and sunny and I jump from my bed full of excited anticipation. It's only seven o'clock and since it's the weekend Mom and Dad aren't up yet. The house is unusually quiet as I dress and tiptoe into the kitchen. I pour myself a bowl of cold cereal with milk and as I eat I wonder if any of the other R*U*1*2s are up yet.

Although Shacoo, Tank and I discussed leaving early enough to grab the first place in line to enter the shuttle, I still have to suppress the urge to call them. Hopefully they're up and preparing to leave. Shacoo was going to go by and pick up Sally.

I finish my cereal and leave a note for my parents telling them I've already headed for the fairgrounds. They'll understand that in my exuberance I'm too excited to wait any longer. I grab the five dollar bill Dad gave me the night before to pay for the four of us and stick it in my pocket.

It's eight o'clock by the time I reach the tour site and I'm just barely ahead of another group as I stake out first place in line. The area is buzzing with activity and soon a long line begins to form. I'm concerned that I haven't seen Shacoo or Tank so I give Shacoo a call.

"Hey, Shacoo," I say when she answers. "I'm here at the fair-grounds in pole position. What's your ETA?"

"Sally and I are about five minutes out. I haven't seen Tank yet, have you?"

"No, but I'm sure he'll be here pretty soon." I no sooner get the words out of my mouth than Tank taps me on the shoulder. "He just arrived," I say. "We'll see you and Sally in a few minutes."

"Roger that," Shacoo says. After five minutes pass I look back and see her wave at me as she and Sally approach. Sally runs up and grabs my hand.

Hi, Genius, I'm just so excited,
That I, too, was invited.

"Of course, we wouldn't think of doing anything like this without you," I say.

I watch Tank roll his eyes. I guess he must be remembering our trip back in time late last summer. Although Sally wasn't directly the cause of the four of us being transported to ancient Egypt and Rome, her little tantrum had a lot to do with creating our dilemma.

I punch Tank on the shoulder. "Relax! Just exactly what do you think could happen here?"

Tank rolls his eyes again indicating with Sally's past history almost anything could happen.

It's getting close to nine o'clock and we huddle together as we wait in line. I examine the shuttle and say, "I read that the authentic shuttle was too large to take on tour but this one is an exact replica only on a smaller scale. From my research, I know the space shuttle has three main compartments which consist of the orbiter which is the part that resembles an airplane, the external tank and the solid rocket boosters. I'm sure the external tank and rocket boosters are fake and only provided to display what the real deal looks like.

"They look real to me," Tank says.

"I also read that the flight deck has large bay windows that allow the crew to see outside. Although the flight deck is equipped with only two seats, one for the pilot and one for the copilot, the seats were expanded for the tour to accommodate four passengers instead of just the two.

"The instrument panels are mind boggling. Some of the equipment is used to execute complex maneuvers for rendezvous, station-keeping, docking, payload deployment/retrieval, robotic arm and bay door operations and of course, closed circuit television operations, just to mention a few. The flight deck's vast display of panels and controls cause one to wonder how anyone can gain the knowledge of how to manipulate the spacecraft."

Before anyone can say more the tour begins. A man dressed in an Air Force uniform approaches the line.

"Ladies, gentlemen and children, too, my name is Major Donahue and I'll be your tour guide. I've been with NASA for ten years and have travelled in outer space on three occasions. I can assure you that you're in for the thrill of a lifetime."

Major Donohue looks toward the shuttle and nods. "It looks as though we're about to begin the tour. It's estimated that each individual group will take approximately fifteen minutes. We realize the line is long and some of the youngsters may get restless.

However, we ask for your patience so that everyone can enjoy the experience. Thank you."

Major Donohue then separates Shacoo, Tank, Sally and me from the line and motions us up a ramp to the entrance of the shuttle. I hand him the five dollar bill. He hands me a one in exchange. My heart is pounding so fast, I wonder why everyone can't hear it. Sally clings to my hand like there's no tomorrow and I notice the excitement on the faces of Shacoo and Tank. As soon as we reach the top of the ramp a door slides open and we're ushered into the interior of the space shuttle. Major Donohue enters with us.

"As you can see, space is limited. The four of you have seats up there," Major Donohue points to the flight deck. "You will be guided through the operations of the spacecraft by another NASA officer. So now if you have no questions, I will leave and turn you over to the narrator. Enjoy the ride!"

I'm spellbound at the sight before me. *Can it be true? Am I really standing here in the cockpit of a real spacecraft?* Before I can say anything the door we came through suddenly slides shut and Major Donohue is gone. My three companions whip around at the sound of the door closing.

"What do we do now?" Tank asks.

"I think we're supposed to take the seats on the flight deck. Come on, we don't want to miss a thing," I say.

In our excitement none of us notice that Sally's shoestring has come untied. The flight deck is slightly elevated and when Sally steps up she trips on an untied shoestring, stumbles and careens forward, falling against the controls. I try to grab her but I'm too late and she lands sprawled across the instrument panel.

I can tell by the expressions on the faces of my companions that they're also stunned.

Oh, my gosh, what did I just do,

I'm so sorry, I tripped over my shoe.

I hope I didn't spoil the fun,

Not only for me, but for everyone.

"Don't fret, Sally," Shacoo says and holds out her hand to help Sally up. "Are you hurt?"

I don't think so,

I just bumped my elbow—

Shacoo and I lift Sally from the panel and as soon as we do we hear a whirling noise that sounds as though it's coming from outside the shuttle.

"What is that?" Tank asks and I notice his voice is trembling.

"Probably the air conditioning," I say and cross my fingers hoping I'm right.

Immediately, the craft starts to shimmy and a voice comes from nowhere. "Take your seats and fasten your harnesses. We seem to have developed a problem and have inadvertently been put into launch mode."

I don't even believe it! Sally? We'll probably be arrested for tampering with government property—that is if we survive.

In our haste and anxiety to follow orders we scramble over each other to our places on the flight deck. I fasten my harness and watch the others struggle with the unfamiliar devices. The whirling sound grows louder so I unfasten my harness and rush to help them. Once they're fastened in I dive into my seat and barely make it before we feel a sudden pull against gravity and the sensation of moving upwards.

Apparently Tank just couldn't pass up the opportunity to razz me. He says, "Wasn't it you who said just a few minutes ago, 'Relax! Just exactly what do you think could happen here?'"

Guess I deserve that jab.

I'm sure Sally overheard Tank's remark. However I think she must also be in shock. She stays still but her eyes tell the story. Tears are creeping down her cheeks. And me? I have no recourse but to stay silent and wait for what no doubt is coming next.

~~~~~~

WE FEEL THE SENSATION of moving away from Earth and we stare out of the wrap around bay window we're seated behind. It appears to me that we're all torn between being fascinated by what's happening before us and the fear of being lost in space forever.

As if on cue that voice from nowhere comes through the loud speakers of the shuttle again. "We have isolated the problem and are working on returning the shuttle to the launch pad. You are in no danger whatsoever and we should have you back down before too much longer."

I look at my fellow *astronauts*. They appear to be more relaxed and reassured by the mystery voice. We are all now excitedly watching the panorama unfolding before our very eyes. Sally is all smiles watching all the dials as their lights herald each phase of the launching process.

CHAPTER TEN
INTO THE WILD BLUE YONDER

We watch Earth grow smaller as we ascend into the wild blue yonder. It boggles the mind when you consider the massive man-made and natural geographic objects that can be seen from hundreds of miles above Earth. I detect some landmarks that I know can be seen from outer space when I realize we are now passing over the Middle East.

When I recognize the Arabian Gulf and Dubai, I shout, "Look! There's Dubai's Palm Island." From our vantage point we can see how the two artificial islands were put together in the shape of a palm tree which is spread across an area of a million cubic meters.

Shacoo strains forward to get a better look. "In English how many miles is that?"

"Don't know exactly. I never bothered to figure it out, but as you can see, it's a lot."

"The island looks like a palm tree," she says, "a huge palm tree. That's incredible! How'd they do that?"

"The construction began in 2001. It was created by dredging sand in the shallow waters off the coast of Dubai," I say. "Three billion cubic feet of sand was brought up from the seafloor and the engineers used the global positioning system to shape the sand into a palm tree with seventeen palm fronds. In addition to all that sand, seven million tons of mountain rock was trucked in and arranged around the coastline to create a breakwater to help protect the inland from waves and storms. The breakwater is seven miles long."

I pause as we all stare out of the bay window admiring the structure many miles below us. "You'll notice the palm fronds appear to be white. That's because of the sand used to design them. The white sand contrasts nicely with the various shades of blue of the surrounding ocean water. Although we can't make out the buildings or other structures from this far up in space I read where many luxury hotels, private villas and exclusive malls grace this man-made wonder."

"Wow," Tank exclaims. "How long did it take to complete?"

"Hum, as I remember it was approximately six years. The island adds about forty-eight miles to Dubai's coastline. The construction has been called by some the *eighth wonder of the world*. Dubai's Palm Islands are made from all natural materials consisting of rock and sand. The ruling prince wanted the islands to appear natural so he insisted they be constructed without the use of concrete or steel. The contractors and engineers worked together and met the challenge head-on." After a pause, I say, "You're looking at the finished project and I read that a Palm address is a status symbol in Dubai."

Genius, what does Palm address mean?
Someplace where everything's green?

I laugh at Sally's question. "Well, you could say that, Sally. But I think a Palm address refers to the color of money and not an abundance of foliage."

~~~~~~~

ALTHOUGH IT'S STILL MORNING in Jefferson City, it's night on the other side of our planet. As we continue to tumble through space we're now on the dark side of Earth. Still staring out of the bay window our attention is drawn below to the lights of what I recognize to be some of the major cities around the globe.

"What's that?" Tank asks without taking his eyes from the window.

"I think it must be the lights of some of the major cities across Europe. I remember reading an article in a magazine that some of the astronauts said in their opinion the cities' lights were among the more impressive visuals from outer space."

We barely have time to appreciate what's unfolding below us before the next phenomenon captures our attention. I'm still reeling from the steady stream of sights passing across our field of vision when the plankton blooms come into view.

> *Oh, look down below,*
> *The ocean is all aglow.*
> *It's purple, pink, yellow and green,*
> *That's something I've never seen.*

I'm almost breathless when I recognize we're actually drifting over the plankton blooms. "Sally, what you're looking at is called the plankton blooms," I say. "Our seventh grade science teacher, Mr. Lawrence, was fascinated with the plankton blooms and spent some time explaining to us their value. They're plants that form in warm ocean water and become food for the smallest of the ocean creatures to the largest of the whales. The blooms are seen as a multi-colored swirl from space. They are considered one of the most stunning phenomenon that occurs in oceans. They consist of uncountable numbers of microscopic plants called phytoplankton. They are also instrumental in transforming carbon dioxide into oxygen. I remember from our science class that photosynthesis is also the process of plants creating oxygen and the importance of phytoplankton is similar to photosynthesis inasmuch as they both create oxygen. And as you know all living things need oxygen to survive."

All of this seems surreal and I can barely take it in. My head is spinning as I try to get a grasp on reality. Even though it feels like we're barely moving I know we must be traveling at least 17,500 miles an hour—the speed required to remain in orbit.

As soon as one spectacular view fades from below us another takes its place. We're now floating above the Pyramids of Giza. When they come into view, looking down upon them takes my breath away.

"Look, there's the pyramids!" Shacoo squeals.

Her eyes are glowing and judging from her excitement I think she must be remembering the day she and Sally were stranded in ancient Egypt when the time machine carnival ride malfunctioned. She told me, after they safely returned to Jefferson City after their wild ride, that someday she was going to visit the pyramids for real.

"The age-old question of how the Egyptians constructed these wonders still remains unanswered," I say. "Did the Egyptians have the help of aliens? No one knows. Perhaps with space travel that question may someday be answered."

I'm secretly hoping we pass over the Colosseum in Rome which I know can be seen from space. I glance over at Tank. He's so absorbed with what's happening on the other side of the wraparound window he doesn't look in my direction. While Shacoo and Sally were stranded in Egypt Tank and I were stranded in ancient Rome. However unlike Tank after that near death experience, I don't have a burning desire to return to Rome.

I'm not sure how our orbit is evolving but suddenly we're back over the United States and viewing the Grand Canyon. I've seen many photographs of the canyon and even been to the Grand Canyon but nothing compares to the view from outer space. We're able to see the canyon from the beginning to the end—all at once. When I think that the Colorado River carved this masterpiece over a span of millions of years, I'm still fascinated.

"How long is the Grand Canyon and how long did it take to form," Tank asks.

"It's two hundred and twenty-seven river miles long and carved entirely by the Colorado River through layers of schist, sandstone, limestone and more. Some researchers say the canyon dates back some seventy million years," I reply.

"Seventy million years! That boggles the mind," Shacoo says.

"Indeed it does. The canyon's South Rim hosts about ninety percent of the five million people that visit the canyon each year. The remote North Rim is approximately one thousand feet higher than the South Rim. The roads to the North Rim are closed, because of weather conditions from October through May and vacationers cannot visit the North Rim during those months.

I strain to see the last view of the canyon as we move deeper into space. I'm now eager for the next experience that awaits us.

CHAPTER ELEVEN
TREK INTO DEEP SPACE

uddenly, it gets extremely dark in our cabin and I sense Sally fidgeting next to me. I take her hand to reassure her and whisper, "It's okay, Sally. Major Donohue and the mystery voice have assured us that everything is under control."

Oh, Genius. I hope it's okay.

I'm so sorry is all I can say...

"Sally, it was an accident. It wasn't your fault you tripped. Just think of all we would have missed if you hadn't launched us. Besides we've been reassured that everything is going to be just fine," I say again and squeeze her hand. Shacoo puts her arm around Sally's shoulder and pulls her close.

Just then the International Space Station (ISS) swims into view. Still harnessed in, we all scoot to the edge of our seats and peer out of the window.

Tank glances at me, "Tell us what you know about the International Space Station," he says.

"Okay," I say and rack my brain for details. "Well, I know the ISS to be the most complex engineering project in the history of mankind. It's a flying U.S. satellite that contains a laboratory and observation platform. It is said to be a stepping stone for further space expeditions.

"The station orbits at an altitude of two hundred and forty-eight miles and circles Earth every ninety minutes. Moving at seventeen thousand five hundred miles per hour, the space station, in one day, could cover the distance that it would take to travel from Earth to the moon and back again. If you know where to look the ISS can be seen from Earth without the use of a telescope. It looks like a bright light moving across the night sky."

"That's incredible," Tank says. "Now you know why I want to be an astronaut instead of a cop."

"What? And disappoint your dad?"

"I haven't told him yet about the career change."

I punch Tank's shoulder. "Better wait until you're sure. You may change your mind a time or two before you make a final decision."

As we float past, we observe an astronaut tethered to the ISS who appears to be working on the outside of the spacecraft. He waves to us, apparently unabashed that four children are manning one of NASA's space shuttles. *Is this a dream or is it really happening?*

"Holy jumpin' Jupiter, did you see that?" Tanks shouts, and his voice swells with excitement.

Before I can answer, I feel our craft turn in a different direction. I'm suddenly caught again between being totally overwhelmed by the spectacle unfolding before us and the fear of how we're going to get back to Earth even though we've been reassured a couple of times we're not in any danger. Not knowing who is in control of our craft, I sense we're at the mercy of the Houston technicians.

Suddenly the mystery voice comes through the cabin again. "We're making progress with your return and will have you back safe and sound in just a little while. In the meantime, if you would like to experience zero gravity, unbuckle your harnesses and see what it feels like to defy gravity and float around the craft for a few minutes."

"Huh! You mean we can do that?" I ask.

"Yes, but just for a few minutes while we, ah, while we adjust your flight plan."

We waste no time and unbuckle our harnesses. Slowly floating upwards, we gently bump into each other as we drift through the capsule. The sensation is much like a carnival ride and we laughingly enjoy the experience.

"Okay team, it's time to retake your seats," mystery voice says. "We're going to be moving through deep space as we direct you back to ground zero."

The four of us make swimming strokes through the cabin and get back into our seats and buckle our harnesses. *I'm not sure I want this experience to end and I agree with Tank regarding a career as an astronaut.*

"Imagine getting paid to do this!" Tank says.

~~~~~~~

AS I GAZE THROUGH the bay window surrounding the flight deck I notice the planets seem to be lining up. That's unusual and I don't know how it's possible as the planets are millions of miles apart. But then again I don't know how it's possible that we find ourselves meandering through deep space.

"I think we're going to take a tour of the planets," I say. "The eight planets that I know are Mercury, Venus, Earth, Mars, Jupiter, Saturn, Neptune and Uranus."

The telescope my parents bought me for Christmas and my passion for the night sky is coming in handy. I'm able to identify each planet as it comes into view and then fades in the distance as we pass. I'm still flabbergasted that we are able to visit all of the planets at the same time because of the distance that separates them. This whole outer space gig is blowing my mind.

Without taking her eyes away from the window, Shacoo asks, "How did the planets get their names?"

I welcome the opportunity to get back on solid ground— back to something logical that I know about. I say, "Well, you see, back when Rome was the center of civilization thousands of years ago, almost everything was named for a Roman or Greek god or goddess. The ancients named all the planets they could see with the naked eye which consisted of Jupiter, Saturn, Mars, Venus and Mercury. Mercury was revered by the Romans as the god of travel. Next time you see a picture of Mercury, notice he has wings on his heels. Venus was and still is the Roman goddess of love and beauty; Mars was the Roman god of war; Jupiter was the king of the Roman gods; Saturn was the Roman god of agriculture; Uranus was the ancient Greek king of the gods, and Neptune was the Roman god of the sea. The other planets were discovered after telescopes were invented but the tradition of naming them after deity remained. Earth is the only planet that is not named for a god. The word Earth is a combination of English and German which simply means *the ground*."

"Yuck!" Shacoo says. "That's kinda disappointing after hearing all the romantic names of the other planets."

"Never thought of it, but now I agree."

"Tell us more," Tank urges.

"Okay. Mercury is the closest planet to the sun. However it orbits from between twenty-nine and seventy million miles from the sun. Which in space could be considered pretty close quarters. Mercury is the smallest of the planets. It's only about two-fifths the size of Earth. And compared to Saturn and Jupiter, Earth is teeny-tiny.

"Venus is the second closest planet to the sun and is nearly the same size as Earth. It orbits closer to Earth than any other planet in outer space. Surprisingly enough, Venus' atmosphere creates the greenhouse effect which makes it the hottest planet in the solar system even though Mercury is closest to the sun.

"Our planet Earth is next in line. We are the third closest to the sun and the only one of the planets known to support life. As we all know, we enjoy twenty-four hour days and it takes Earth three hundred and sixty-five days to circle the sun. It is believed that Earth is the first planet to have a moon. Scholars contend that our moon was created when a large body, such as an asteroid, collided with Earth thus ejecting massive amounts of Earth's substance. This substance collected in a ball in space and orbited eventually creating our moon.

"Our neighbor, Mars, has always intrigued me, maybe because of stories about Martians and life on planet Mars. Mars is fourth in line from the sun positioned next to Earth. It is also known as the red planet simply because it appears to be red."

As we continue to watch the melodrama unfold before our eyes, Mars comes into view. I lean across the control panel and try to press my face against the window to get a good look. I find it hard to believe we're actually flying around the universe as if we were watching some slideshow.

As we grow closer to Mars, we seem to be slowing down. When we glide past Mars, I see three flying saucers whiz past us and imagine green creatures staring back at us from the windows in their crafts. I shake my head trying to figure out what is real and what is not.

"I think I'm losing it," I mutter.

"No, you…you're not," Shacoo stammers, "I saw them, too."

"And so did I," Tank whispers.

Sally grabs my hand.

> *Did you just see green men fly past?*
> *I wasn't sure, they went so fast.*
> *Am I seeing things?*
> *Or, were those real beings?*

"Not sure," is all I manage to say. I'm still trying to grasp all that is happening. I know the mind plays tricks and I'm trying to separate fact from fiction.

I don't have time to dwell on the prospect that we just saw three flying saucers manned by little green men buzz by us because planet Jupiter is rapidly coming into view. I recognize Jupiter from the great red spot that the planet is known for. I remember reading that it takes Jupiter twelve years to orbit the sun. It takes our planet only one year. Jupiter is the largest of the eight planets, even larger than Saturn.

Gazing out into space, I'm stunned when I see a planet that looks like Saturn appear in the window of the flight deck. I recognize Saturn by its rings. It's the sixth planet from the sun and is nine and one-half times larger than Earth. Mr. Lawrence taught us that by using the first letter of each planet's name and making up a sentence, we can easily remember how the planets line up from the sun. His sentence was: *My Very Excellent Mother Just Served Us Noodles.* The first letter in each word lines up the planets as Mercury, Venus, Earth, Mars, Jupiter, Saturn, Uranus and Neptune.

As we drift closer, Saturn suddenly fills the entire window and it looks to me as though we're going to crash into the massive planet.

"Duck," I shout, and push Sally's head down.

The four of us huddle together waiting for the collision. After a few moments when no crash occurs, I take a chance and look out again. We've made a half-circle around Saturn and are speeding off in another direction. I breathe a sigh of relief and notice the others staring out of the window as well. I'm still too frightened to speak, so we just sit in stunned silence.

Again the mystery voice from nowhere fills the shuttle. "Whew! That was close. But do not fear we have control of the situation and no harm will come to you."

I'm shaking in my shoes and notice my companions are too. *Maybe I'll give mystery voice a piece of my mind if and when we return to Earth.*

Continuing through space, we make a pass by Neptune and Uranus. These two planets are similar in size and are estimated to have a mass seventeen times the size of Earth. Uranus orbits the sun only once every one hundred and sixty-five years. Neptune is so far from the sun that it has only one percent of the sunlight that Earth enjoys. Neptune has three rings surrounding it and astronomers think the rings were formed when one of Neptune's moons was destroyed. I keep recounting what I learned in school and from reading *National Geographic.*

~~~~~~~

OUR RIDE IS SHIFTING and I sense that because we've visited all the planets we're going in another direction. I hear Sally ask Shacoo:

> We've been all the way to Mars,
> Still we've seen no little cars

Where's the man they put in orbit?

He's my all-time favorite.

"You mean Starman?" Shacoo asks. "You never know when he'll pass this way in his midnight cherry roaster."

I'll keep a look

Maybe someday I'll write a book.

CHAPTER TWELVE
DANCING WITH THE STARS

Although the planets are fascinating, I'm hoping we also get to tour stars and constellations. Ever since my parents gave me a telescope for my tenth birthday I've been intrigued by the night sky. The ancients thought certain groups of stars looked like their gods or outlines of animals. I admit sometimes I had to stretch my imagination to make the stars fit the description. I've been told that the sole purpose for naming and describing the constellations was to help people on Earth tell which stars were which. This theory also makes sense because sailors of yore used the stars to navigate their ships across the uncharted seas.

Suddenly my wish to visit the stars is granted as I observe the galaxy of stars known as the Milky Way come into view.

"What's that?" Tank asks not taking his eyes away from the wraparound window.

"That's the great Milky Way. It's been estimated to contain from two hundred billion to four hundred billion stars."

"WOW! Tank says. "No wonder it's called the great Milky Way."

"Yes, and even so the Milky Way is only a tiny portion of the entire heavenly universe," I say. "There are trillions of celestial objects visible at night. Although my telescope doesn't come close to seeing what the massive telescopes located in observatories around the world do, it does a pretty good job. I can pick out some of the most well-known stars."

Oh, Genius, that's so cool,
Did you learn all that in school?

"Well, Sally, most of it I learned from studying the night sky and referring to books and charts. You may have heard of NASA's Hubble Space Telescope. It was launched into space in 1990 from the shuttle Discovery much like your hero Spaceman. He was launched from Falcon, SpaceX's rocket. The Hubble telescope has been orbiting Earth for twenty six years sending back incredible images of space."

You mean traveling the same way we are?
I won't last twenty-six years or travel that far.

"Don't worry, Sally. I believe Sergeant Donohue is going to get us back to Earth before much longer." *At least I hope so.*

As we continue to roam around the galaxy, I recognize Polaris in the distance. Polaris is better known as the North Star. "Look, there's the North Star," I say.

"Oh, for sure," Shacoo says. "That's my favorite one. From my bedroom window I can see it in the sky and I look for the North Star every night."

"It's pretty easy to spot. It's the star closest to the north celestial pole."

"What's the north celestial pole?" Tank asks.

"Well, Tank, the north and south *celestial* poles are only imaginary points. They signify the axis of Earth's rotation. All stars seen from the northern hemisphere rotate from the north celestial pole. Because of the North Star's location in the sky it has been used by wayfarers for centuries to help navigate them across the oceans."

"Genius, you truly are a genius," Shacoo says.

"Thank you. I've always been intrigued by the sky. Oh, look, now we can see Sirius. Sirius is also known as the Dog Star…"

Dog Star? How can that be?
It doesn't look like a dog to me!

"Well, Sally you see, the ancients had pretty good imaginations. The Greeks associated the rising of Sirius as a sign that the dog days of summer were upon them and it usually heralded in the flooding of the Nile River."

What does dog days of summer mean?
This is stuff I've never seen.

I scratch my head searching for an answer that Sally would understand. "The dog days refer to the hottest part of summer. That's usually between July to mid-August," I say and rush on before Sally can ask another question. "Sirius is the brightest star in the night sky. Even the name Sirius, a derivative from the Greek word Seirios, means glowing or scorcher—much like our Iowa summers."

Suddenly the view from our window begins to change. Everything below is starting to look familiar.

"What's going on, Genius?" Tank asks.

"I think Houston has succeeded in returning us to Earth." I'm elated to be home but saddened to leave the exciting adventure of traveling in space.

OUR SPACECRAFT COMES TO an abrupt halt and the doors at the rear of the cabin slide open. Sergeant Donohue and another man dressed in a space suit enter.

"Hello, crew," the other man says. "I'm Captain Neilson. We hope you enjoyed your trek into space."

"Oh, yes," I say, "we did indeed. But how…how did all of that happen? I don't quite understand how we were able to launch this spacecraft?"

Sergeant Donohue takes the lead. "As you all probably know secrecy is important to national security. We are entrusting you with a highly guarded secret—in fact it's Top Secret!"

I'm thrilled to think NASA would trust children like us with a top secret. I look at Shacoo, Tank and Sally. They're staring wide-eyed at the two men. I think we're all too dumbstruck to speak.

Sergeant Donohue continues, "You did take a trip into outer space but not the way you thought. Everything you saw was prerecorded on a videotape. The spacecraft is programmed to make movements that correspond with the video at the appropriate time. That's why you felt like you were turning and spinning in space. When you thought you were launched that's when the ride started and simulated a trip into outer space." Sergeant Donohue then looks at Sally, "You're off the hook, Sally. You didn't cause the launch."

I didn't? That's a relief.
I was scared beyond belief.

"How can that be?" I ask. "It was much too real to be fake."

"Thank you! We strive for perfection," Captain Neilson says with a broad smile. "Now you have to do your part."

I notice my companions perk up. "Yes, Sir!" I say, answering for all of us.

"We have a line of your friends and neighbors waiting out there," Captain Neilson says. "In order for all of them to experience what you just did, we request that you not tell our secret until everyone has had a turn to enjoy the thrill of space travel."

Oh, my, that's going to be fun.

I won't ruin it for anyone.

"Nor will I," Shacoo says and hugs Sally.

"Tank and I want to be astronauts. You can count on us to keep the secret," I say and Tank vigorously nods his head.

"Wonderful! I think all four of you would be an asset to the space program," Sergeant Donohue says. He then reaches into a cardboard box he was carrying and hands each of us a small gift box. They have the NASA logo imprinted on the outside. "These are for you to keep as a reminder of your trip into the fascinating world of outer space."

"Thank you, Sir," we all say in unison.

"You're welcome," Sergeant Donohue says. "Come this way," and he then escorts us out of the shuttle.

Once we're back on solid ground and away from those in line waiting their turn, we huddle together and open our boxes. Inside we find a small block of wood supporting a glass sphere. The sphere has a replica of *our* spacecraft suspended in the center. The block of wood is inscribed:

To those brave souls who are daring

enough to explore unknown universes.

May your thirst for adventure never run dry.

The name, *Intrepid,* is painted in tiny letters on the side of the small replica of the spacecraft.

"Intrepid," I whisper and am overcome with emotion. Sally takes my hand,

What does that word mean, Genius?

Something to do with the four of us?

I think back to some of our past adventures before answering. We helped capture two criminals we called *The Cat* and *The Wiesel*. We rescued a four-year old Cuban refugee we named *Blue*. We befriended the spirit of Lucinda Bradbury and helped save Bradbury Mansion from being torn down. We managed to return Snow White and Little Red Riding Hood to their proper places in the fairytales after Sally materialized them. When we were accidentally sent back in time to ancient Egypt and Rome, we managed to return home safely. And we were able to decipher Shacoo's treasure map and find the hidden treasure.

"Sally, the word intrepid means fearless, unafraid, adventurous, bold, daring and spirited. Yes, I think it does apply to the *R*U*1*2s.*"

WHEN I ARRIVE HOME, I place the glass sphere on my nightstand. Now every night before I turn out the light I ponder the wonders of space. If there was ever any reluctance as to my resolve to become an astronaut, especially after our trip aboard the *Intrepid*, it's vanished into thin air.

CHAPTER THIRTEEN
JOHNSON SPACE CENTER

'll never forget the day Dad came home from the clinic and announced this year's medical convention was going to be held in Houston, Texas. It was a hot mid-July summer day and I was playing fetch with RX, my pet Siberian Husky when Dad drove up. He sat down in the shade on the front steps and called to me.

"Genius, come sit for a minute. I have something I want to tell you."

"Hi, Dad," I respond and coax RX to come with me as I join Dad on the steps.

"Hey, boy," Dad says as he ruffles RX's head with both hands. RX is in doggie heaven. He rolls over on his back anticipating a tummy rub. Dad doesn't disappoint. He gives RX a good rub-down and then shoos him away. "Go on now. I have something important to talk to your master about." RX stands and shakes himself before loping around to the back of the house.

"What is it, Dad?" I ask wondering if I'm in trouble.

"How'd you like to go to Houston?"

"Houston, Texas!" I shout. "Where the Space Center is located?"

"One and the same," Dad answers. "This year's medical convention is being held there and Mom and I are going to attend." Dad pauses for a moment. "We thought you might like to go—"

"OH, BOY, OH, BOY!" I say and jump up. "Would I ever!"

"Thought you might. And you don't even have to ask. Of course Tank can go if his parents approve."

I waste no time and pull my cellphone from my hip pocket as I watch Dad go into the house shaking his head.

"Hello," Tank answers.

"Tank, you're not going to believe this but...but...we've been invited to go to Houston."

After a slight pause, Tank says, "Not funny, Genius. I'm very serious about becoming an astronaut and don't appreciate you joking about it."

"No joke! The national medical convention is in Houston this year and Mom and Dad are attending. I'm going and they said I could invite you but if you're not interested—"

I hear a crash before Tank comes back. "Sorry, I got so excited I dropped my phone," he says. "How soon are we leaving?"

"I forgot to ask. I'll get the details. In the meantime, you get permission."

~~~~~~~

COMPARED TO OUR TRIP into space the flight to Houston is boring. Tank and I sat across the aisle from Mom and Dad and take turns trading out the window seat.

Watching out the window I feel a pang of guilt when I remember how excited Shacoo was when we took the space shuttle ride and how disappointed she acted when she learned that Tank and I were going to Houston. I ask Tank, "Do you think Shacoo will ever get over it?"

"Aw, I think so. She's not one to hold a grudge. Disappointed but not disgruntled. After our adventure at sea she probably thought it was her turn."

"She should be happy she didn't have to endure that ordeal. Besides, you and I have made a career choice. Think she's probably had enough outer space exploration to last for a while. Not sure she would like to be an astronaut."

"Okay, Genius. You go convince her why she wasn't invited. You could talk an Eskimo into buying more snow."

<hr/>

WHEN WE LAND IN Houston we take the shuttle to the Lone Star Hotel. Tank and I have a room adjoining Mom and Dad's on the twentieth floor. My parents will be busy all three days attending the convention. However we're informed that the hotel has a bus that goes to the space center twice daily. The desk clerk advises my parents that the bus tours are closely monitored and the drivers are government employees from the space center. He said it wasn't unusual for children over the age of ten to take the bus unaccompanied by adults.

After exacting promises from Tank and me that we will use every precaution and be safe, my parents agree that we can take the bus tour.

After lunch Tank and I join the line from the hotel waiting for the space center bus to arrive.

"Pinch me! I just can't believe we're actually going to the space center," I say.

"If I'm sleeping, don't wake me up," Tank replies. "Thank you for giving me the opportunity to come with you. You know how much this means to me."

"To both of us! Wouldn't do it without you," I say and Tank and I exchange a knuckle bump.

Once we're all aboard our bus driver introduces himself as Marty and our tour guide as Samantha. He says that both he and Samantha have applied to the space program and someday hope to be astronauts. One of the passengers boldly asks what it takes to become an astronaut.

"It isn't easy," Marty says. "There are a large number of applicants and NASA accepts only the very best. Only a fraction of one percent make it into the space training program. In addition to a bachelor's degree in engineering, biological science, physical science or math, you must have no less than three years of related professional experience or one thousand commander pilot hours on a jet. In addition your vision must be twenty-twenty in each eye."

"Guess we know now what we have to do to make it there from here," I whisper to Tank.

Tank grunts. "I know *you* can do it, but not sure I can."

"If you want it bad enough, you can. All it takes is commitment and hard work. Since we have to become a jet pilot first, we have plenty of time to think about it."

WHEN WE APPROACH THE Johnson Space Center the first thing we see is the six-story tall exhibit of the modified 747 airplane with the space shuttle mounted on top. This display is the only shuttle replica in the world that is mounted on the original aircraft. The purpose of the plane is to ferry the shuttle from place to place.

"Just look at that!" Tank exclaims. "The747 is a lot bigger than I thought. Imagine flying that with the shuttle riding piggy-back."

"I know. It boggles my mind that something as large as an airplane can even get off the ground, much less take flight carrying something on top as big as the shuttle."

Samantha directs our attention to points of interest as the bus passes. She tells us that the Johnson Space Center is the home of Mission Control and astronaut training." She says, "Since its opening in 1992, there have been more than a million visitors each year." She then says, "There are more than four hundred space artifacts and exhibits, including live shows and theaters."

We go to the Starship Gallery where we see artifacts of the first space crafts. Included are the Mercury 9 and Gemini 5 space capsules. Also on display are Apollo 17 and of course my favorite, Skylab.

Tanks eyes light up when we're shown Apollo 17. "Can you believe we're looking at the actual space shuttle that has been to the moon and back?" he asks.

"Amazing!" I say. "Let's go look at some of the moon rocks it brought back from its epoch journey."

When we examine the rocks, Tank says, "Looks like the rocks that erupted from Mt. St. Helens."

"Can't believe all those came from the moon. How do you suppose they were loaded on the shuttle?"

"Guess if you dropped one they'd float off into outer space."

"And from there where?"

Samantha is busy answering other visitors' questions so we don't get a chance to ask ours before we're off again. Guess we'll have plenty of time later to find the answers. However, we do pick up some brochures to take home to show Shacoo and the other R*U*1*2s.

I remember reading that Skylab was designed to explore how space flight affected human flight into space. The astronauts aboard Skylab conducted experiments in the fields of space physics, geophysics, micro-gravity biomedical and biological studies and micro-gravity technology research. High school students' projects were also carried out on Skylab in order to promote interest in space. Skylab was not called a space station as is today's International Space Station. Instead, it was referred to as an orbital workshop. It orbited Earth from 1973 to 1979. In 1979 Skylab fell to earth and in 1998 the ISS, International Space Station, was launched and is still orbiting.

We take the open air tram tour and visit Rocket Park where we see three of the actual Saturn V rockets on display. These rockets helped propel space exploration. We are allowed to take a walk on the path through the Space Vehicle Mockup Facility. This is where astronauts train for current missions. We also visit the Mission Operations Control Room. Some of the equipment looks much like the dashboard on *Intrepid*. We also toured Mission Control where all of the launches, including the International Space Station, are monitored.

"WOW! Genius, look at that," Tank says. "Kinda wish our ride had been the real thing after seeing all of this."

"Me, too," I reply. "Looks like it's gonna take a lot of hard work before we can even think of becoming an astronaut. Guess grade school, high school and college are not such a waste after all."

I'm sad when Samantha announces that our tour is near an end. Our last visit is a tour of the Mission Mars exhibit. This mission focuses on future travel to Mars.

Maybe I'll be the one to man that spacecraft.

THE CHILDHOOD LEGENDS® SERIES

BY JUDITH BLEVINS & CARROLL MULTZ

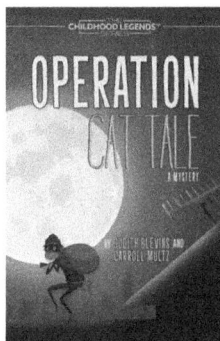

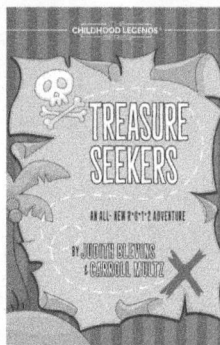

OPERATION CAT TALE
A MYSTERY
BY JUDITH BLEVINS AND CARROLL MULTZ

ONE FRIGHTFUL DAY
A MYSTERY
BY JUDITH BLEVINS & CARROLL MULTZ

BLUE
BEING DISCOVERED WAS NOT AN OPTION...
BY JUDITH BLEVINS & CARROLL MULTZ

THE GHOST OF BRADBURY MANSION
BY JUDITH BLEVINS & CARROLL MULTZ
AN R*U*1*2 ADVENTURE

WHITE OUT
A MAGICAL ADVENTURE FEATURING THE R*U*1*2 GANG
BY JUDITH BLEVINS & CARROLL MULTZ

A FLASH OF RED
A MAGICAL ADVENTURE FEATURING THE R*U*1*2 GANG
BY JUDITH BLEVINS & CARROLL MULTZ

BACK IN TIME
BY JUDITH BLEVINS & CARROLL MULTZ

TREASURE SEEKERS
AN ALL-NEW R*U*1*2 ADVENTURE
BY JUDITH BLEVINS & CARROLL MULTZ

THE ENTIRE R*U*1*2 COLLECTION IS AVAILABLE IN SOFTCOVER & EBOOK AT BOOKSELLERS EVERYWHERE

ABOUT THE AUTHORS

Judith Blevins' whole professional life has been centered in and around the courts and the criminal justice system. Her experience in having been a court clerk and having served under five consecutive district attorneys in Grand Junction, Colorado, has provided the fodder for her novels. She has had a daily dose of mystery, intrigue and courtroom drama over the years and her novels share all with her readers. In addition to the novels in *The Childhood Legends Series*®, she has authored or co-authored ten adult novels.

Carroll Multz, a trial lawyer for over forty years, a former two-term district attorney, assistant attorney general, and judge, has been involved in cases ranging from municipal courts to and including the United States Supreme Court. His high-profile cases have been reported in the *New York Times*, *Redbook Magazine* and various police magazines. He was one of the attorneys in the Columbine Copycat Case that occurred in Fort Collins, Colorado, in 2001 that was featured by Barbara Walters on *ABC's 20/20*. He recently retired as an Adjunct Professor at Colorado Mesa University in Grand Junction, Colorado, where he taught law-related courses at both the graduate and undergraduate levels for twenty-eight years. In addition to the novels in *The Childhood Legends Series*®, he has authored or co-authored twelve adult novels and seven books of non-fiction.

CPSIA information can be obtained
at www.ICGtesting.com
Printed in the USA
FSHW01n0217070918

9 781947 727724